NIGHT IN IRELAND

RICHARD WAKE

MANOR AND STATE, LLC

Copyright © 2025 by Manor and State, LLC

All rights reserved.

No part of this book may be reproduced in any form or by any electronic or mechanical means, including information storage and retrieval systems, without written permission from the author, except for the use of brief quotations in a book review.

This is a work of fiction. All incidents and dialogue, and all characters with the exception of some well-known historical figures, are products of the author's imagination and are not to be construed as real. Where real-life historical figures appear, the situations, incidents, and dialogues concerning those persons are entirely fictional and are not intended to depict actual events or to change the entirely fictional nature of the work. In all other respects, any resemblance to actual persons, living or dead, events, or locales is entirely coincidental.

SIGN UP FOR MY READING GROUP AND RECEIVE A FREE NOVELLA!

I'd love to have you join my on my writing journey. In addition to receiving my newsletter, which contains news about my upcoming books, you'll also receive a FREE novella. Its title is *Ominous Austria*, and it is a prequel to my first series.

The main character, Alex Kovacs, is an everyman who is presented with an opportunity to make a difference on the eve of the Nazis' takeover of Austria. But what can one man do? It is the question that hangs over the entire series, taking Alex from prewar Austria to the Cold War, from Vienna, to Switzerland, to France, and to Eastern Europe.

To receive *Ominous Austria*, as well as the newsletter, click here:

https://dl.bookfunnel.com/g6ifz027t7

PART I

1

The Rhine Cocktail was the drink that year, for some inexplicable reason. I was probably making 50 of them a night. It meant, among other things, having a half-dozen bottles of Champagne chilling in ice buckets under the bar. If I managed not to kick over one of them during my shift, I considered it a successful night.

The Rhine Cocktail: one ounce of brandy — they all wanted Asbach Uralt — followed by one ounce of Cointreau Triple Sec and a half-ounce of Prunella, a particular vile bit of business. Mix that mess together with a dash of bitters and then spoil some perfectly fine Champagne by pouring it over the top to fill the glass. Voilà, the Rhine Cocktail.

"Drinking water from the river itself out of a rubber boot would taste better," I said to Alfred Greschner. He had come for a refill of his club soda glass. He was behind the bar and getting it himself, which was fine, seeing as how he owned the place.

"Don't account for their taste..." Alfred said.

"...just count their money," I said, completing the old man's favorite couplet.

Greschner owned the hotel where I worked, The Denkler. It

was in Heringsdorf, right across the promenade from the beach and the Baltic. There was a time when the kaisers vacationed there but, well, let's just say that five-plus years after the second war, both the kaisers and the hotel had seen better days. The Denkler was south of luxurious, north of a rat trap, but trending more toward the feral every day. There were enough blotches on the lobby carpet that it was no longer possible to cover all of them with chairs and end tables. If you got a room without at least some hint of a stain on the wallpaper, it was like you won the lottery.

But we were still pretty busy, creeping decrepitude and all. The bar took up the entire back end of the lobby — 18 seats plus 10 tables besides. I was pretty sure that we were the true profit center of the operation, given that you could only charge so much for a schnitzel or a room with stained wallpaper. Alcohol, though, was different. As Alfred said, "Even a small mark-up gets multiplied, and the multiplication gets easier and easier as the evening progresses."

"Who taught you that? One of the finance ministers who used to stay here in the 1920s?"

"Alex, my boy, you don't learn about the hotel business in books. But there was this finance minister under Weimar who would come in here for a week every July and never leave that last seat at the end of the bar. I asked him how he liked the beach once and he said, 'Too sandy.' I could have asked him a dozen follow-up questions but I never did."

"Just poured him a dozen more drinks instead?"

"You're learning," Alfred said, and then he was off, heading for the office behind the desk where the guests checked in.

"Alex, my man," said a voice behind me. I turned and smiled reflexively while I searched my memory for his name. Given that this was East Germany, Communist East Germany, we catered to a rather limited clientele — national and regional party officials, big men in the military, people like that. Business was steady but it came from that small pool of swells. I had worked the bar for about 18 months and I was seeing the same faces for a second or third time.

"Herr... Grundmann," I said, snatching the name out of somewhere at the last second.

"Ah, you remember."

"How could I forget one of my best customers," I said. The truth was, he was just like all the rest — a little pasty-faced, a little bossy, trying to relax for a few days but genetically incapable. Grundmann was one of the regional party officials.

"Dresden, right?" I said.

"Very good memory, Alex."

"But I forget your drink."

"I'm feeling adventurous," he said, pointing to the Rhine Cocktail I had just made.

"Adventurous it is," I said. My opinion of the man dropped by about 50 percent as I mixed another.

It was a busy night in the restaurant, and I was working alone, which meant there was a steady flow of waitresses and waiters standing at the end of the bar with drink chits in their hands and annoyance on their faces. I was doing the best I could, serving both the bar customers and the restaurant people, but there was always a tension between say, 8 and 9:30. How quickly I served the bar patrons affected my tips. How quickly I served the waiters and waitresses affected their tips. I really didn't play favorites and alternated between the two clienteles but, well, there was always that tension.

"Come on, Alex, it's just two glasses of Riesling," Heidi said. She was the oldest waitress and the least likely to tolerate even the slightest delay on my end.

"Calm down, dearest Heidi," I said.

"You're too calm. That's your problem."

"Patience is a virtue."

"I'm too old for virtue."

"Is that a proposition?"

"Your heart couldn't take it."

"I'm intrigued."

"Just keep your hands out of your pockets and pour the Riesling," she said.

I liked Heidi. The truth was, I liked most everybody at The Denkler and most everything about the job. I worked nights, carried none of it home with me, slept late, and met some interesting people in the process. Some assholes, too, but assholes could be interesting in their own way.

Take Grundmann, the party hack from Dresden. He was the kind who bullied the kids who worked for the bellman, criticizing them for being slow, treating them as personal manservants when he wanted a newspaper or a glass of water or some such thing. I caught Roddy, one of the kids, giving Grundmann the finger after he'd turned his back. When I asked him about it later, Roddy shrugged and said, "I think I give them all the finger after they turn their backs."

"Nothing special, then?"

"Garden variety jerk," he said.

But, on this night, Herr Grundmann revealed another side of his personality, one that I had not noticed on his previous visit. He did it when he joined, at one of the tables in the darkest corner of the lobby, a young man named Ricky. He was in his early twenties, fit and handsome, and an employee of the hotel along with his sister, Michaela. Ricky and Micky.

"Not exactly employees — I mean, they pay me, after all," Alfred Greschner told me after I saw Ricky handing him an envelope. Every hotel bar needs a hooker, apparently, and Micky and Ricky were ours. Micky took care of the fellas and Ricky took care of either the fellas or the ladies, depending on what was needed. Mostly, it was the fellas. Micky and Ricky paid Grundmann for exclusive rights to work the lobby bar, and they were making enough that Ricky said they were two years away from having enough money to realize their dream of opening a clam shack along the water.

"There's a joke in there somewhere," I said, when Ricky told me. He sometimes sat at the bar and chatted on slow nights.

"Micky's a little shy about the whole thing, and I get it, but the way I figure it, there's no difference between driving a tractor," and then he mimicked a guy steering the thing with two hands, "and pitching hay," and then he made like he was doing that, "and, well..."

And then Ricky smiled and pantomimed in the time-honored, teenaged boy manner, pretending to insert something into his mouth and puffing his cheek out, again and again and again.

"It's all the same in the worker's paradise," he said. I actually spit out my drink and laughed when he did it.

And anyway, on that night, Grundmann from Dresden was sitting with Ricky in the darkest corner of the lobby. And then Ricky left him at the table by himself and walked up the steps next to the front desk. And then, five minutes later, Grundmann from Dresden found himself walking up the same steps. I committed the name and the date to memory and did my best not to wonder who was going to be riding whose tractor up in the second-floor room that Ricky and Micky received as a part of their arrangement with my boss.

2

Lotte was five years old, five going on fifteen — a bit of a tomboy most of the time but capable of feminine wiles when the situation warranted. Those times mostly involved the expenditure of money for a bottle of soda or a pack of gum or some such thing. "Please, please, please," she would say, each word about an octave higher than the previous, and I caved in every time. But that was relatively infrequent. Mostly, we kicked a football back and forth in the small backyard behind Karin's house before dinner.

After we ate, Karin would give Lotte a bath and I would sit in the comfortable chair and read the newspaper, the picture of family contentment. We weren't a family, of course. Karin's husband had died a year or so after the war ended in a Soviet labor camp, leaving her and Lotte to fend for themselves. Karin taught school in Ahlbeck, the little town next to Heringsdorf. My apartment was a block away from their house. We met in the market on Kaiserstrasse when I teased Lotte that the cornsilk was the same color as her hair. That had been nearly a year before.

If it was my night off, as this was, I would stay over after

Lotte went to bed. On those nights, I would make up a story about some faraway place that I had visited to help get her to sleep. I managed to avoid telling her, though, about my uncle being murdered by Nazis in Cologne, or my wife dying in a Resistance airplane crash in Lyon, or the bombs in Paris, or the treachery in Istanbul, or the killings in Budapest, Bucharest, Limoges and the rest. Mine were all happy stories filled with knights and princesses and happily ever after, and I managed to use almost all of the places I had visited over the years. All except Krakow.

"Tell me the one about the boat to Finland," Lotte said, and I tucked her in and began a tale about taking the small boat across the Gulf of Finland, from Estonia to Helsinki. In my telling, it was my job to save a damsel who was trapped in a fort on Suomenlinna, a small island in Helsinki's harbor, and I managed the rescue without even drawing my weapon. I left out the real-life part about the unrepentant Nazis who I ended up shooting on the beach.

Anyway, with the damsel now safe on the boat back to Estonia, Lotte said, "Another one, Alex. Just one more."

"Nope, you know the rules," I said. It was the only time I was ever firm with her, mostly because Karin was in the next room, listening. Lotte would put on a pouting face, but it was just part of the act. I would lean over and kiss her on the forehead, and she would turn on her side, contented.

"I never figured Estonia for one of the greatest hits," Karin said. I had gotten into bed next to her.

"Me neither. I always thought she'd go for the whole Paris bit the best — the lights, the boats on the Seine, the damsel trapped in the Eiffel Tower."

"There's always a damsel in these stories, Mr. Kovacs. I'm not sure what to think about your past sometimes."

I shrugged and said, "The way I figure it, you can't have a

story without a damsel." Then we shucked off what was left of our underclothes. A few minutes later, after I regained my breath, we lay together in the dark, propped up on pillows folded in two. A single shaft of moonlight sneaked through the curtains, bisecting the both of us about waist level.

"When does school start?"

"Two weeks."

"So fast."

"I know, but I'm ready," Karin said. "It's the most fulfilling part of my life."

"Thanks."

"You know what I mean," she said, after punching me in the shoulder.

"Yeah, I do," I said.

Vienna, Zurich, Normandy, Prague. Nazis, Commies. Spy, Resistance fighter, spy again. More good marks in the copy book than bad — a lot more, if I could find it in my heart to be honest with myself. But it was the bad marks that crowded out the rest, the bad marks and the bodies.

"Lotte's not going to be in your class, right?"

"No, no," Karin said. "She'll be in the kindergarten this year, right next door to my school. I'll have third and fourth grade."

"Terrorists," I said.

"I think sixth and seventh grade are the true terrorists. Mine are more terrorists in training. But that's only sometimes. They're actually pretty sweet. Lot of crushes from the little boys."

"I can take them. I'm more worried about the little boys' fathers."

"Not as many fathers as you'd think," she said. And it was true. I always had to remind myself, now that I was living in Germany, what a toll the war had taken on the male population.

Karin drifted off to sleep soon after, and I stared at the ceiling. On a night when the moon was a little brighter, I could count the cracks. There were 17 little spidery fingers, nine to the left of the overhead light fixture and eight to the right. I would fall asleep eventually, and actually sleep pretty well once I did. But it could take an hour, sometimes even more. It could take 15 minutes for me even to screw up the courage to close my eyes.

This night, Karin turned over and caught me, eyes open.

"You still can't relax," she said.

"Not so bad."

"It's been, what, two years?"

"I've only known you for about 10 months."

"You know what I mean."

"Yeah, two years," I said.

It was actually two years, six months, and three days, but Karin didn't need to know that.

3

In Krakow, the Jews mostly lived in Kazimierz. Well, that was before the war. Kazimierz was south of the old town but on the same side of the Vistula River. It was a classic old Jewish neighborhood. It was before the war, anyway.

My meeting with Hyman was in Debniki, though, a neighborhood on the other side of the Vistula. We had a regular meeting on Thursday nights. Debniki was more of an industrial area, but only kind of — there were plenty of parks and lots of vacant land, too. But our meeting was in an empty warehouse that would not have survived a strong gust of wind from the north. Thursdays, 10 p.m.

Hyman lived in Kazimierz, one of the few Jews who survived. He had been sent to Plaszow, the local camp, and then to Auschwitz — but he had lived, somehow. Not that he talked about it. I only knew about the Auschwitz part because Fritz had told me before the start of the mission. He had said, "He's solid, Hyman Pietroski. You survive Auschwitz, you're solid."

"You've met him?"

"Obviously not."

"Then how..."

"You survive Auschwitz, I mean, you've seen some shit."

Nightmare in Poland

"So, you just assume..."

"A pretty safe assumption," Fritz said.

And he was right — Hyman was solid. Nervous, but solid. The truth was, I liked nervous. In my experience with civilian volunteers, the nervous ones were the ones who survived. The confident ones were the problem, when their confidence bled over the line into cockiness. Nervous was good. Cocky was often dead.

It was supposed to be a two-month mission but after six weeks we were about done. Hyman was going to bring the last of the documents to the meeting that night in the warehouse, and that would be that. I had already checked the train schedule for the next morning. It would take two weeks of dinky local trains — the security police didn't bother with those, only the intercity trains — and night crossings through the woods, and miles of walking, but I could still see my flat in Vienna when I closed my eyes.

I set out from the old town at eight. The walk to Debniki wouldn't take an hour, but there was a bar near the warehouse where I could stop. It was the kind of night when I jammed my hands just a little deeper into my pockets, when I pulled down my watch cap to cover my ear lobes, when I entertained myself trying to blow smoke rings with my warm breath. Cold night. Final night.

I warmed up in the bar with a couple of vodkas. I didn't like the stuff that much, but it was what everyone else drank — vodka shot, beer chaser — and I was nothing if not amenable. Alcohol was alcohol in the end, after all — and the last thing I wanted to do was stand out in the crowd. Not that I would, not in that place. It was a venue for serious drinkers avoiding whoever was or wasn't waiting for them at home. Serious drinkers, all men, little conversation. From 20 feet away, you could hear the hum of the refrigerator behind the bar.

At a little after 9:30 I went back outside into the cold and walked the quarter-mile to the warehouse. For our previous meetings, I had always arrived early and waited in some bushes across the street from the entrance. I would wait and watch Hyman arrive, and do my best to make sure that he hadn't been followed, and then join him inside. And the first five times, that was exactly how it had played out.

This time, though, Hyman was late. He tended to show up right around 10, never later than 10:05. But 10:05 became 10:10, and 10:10 became 10:15, and Hyman wasn't there. I was freezing, and needed a piss, and thought for a second amid the rising steam as I let loose in the bushes. Maybe he had been early. That was the most likely explanation, even if he had never been early before. I didn't want to consider the alternative, that he had been found out and snatched and, oh hell. I forced the thought out of my head and looked at my watch: 10:19. Regardless of the explanation, I was going to have to go inside and check. There was no way around that.

I crept out of the bushes, crossed the little street, and headed to the left side of the warehouse instead of the front entrance. It really was dilapidated, and there was half of a board missing from the siding, and I could peer inside through the opening — but it was dark, and there was nothing I could see. I pressed my ear up against the opening and heard nothing. Then I remembered the watch cap and lifted it to expose my ear. Still nothing.

I probably waited for five more minutes, alternately peeking through the opening and listening. Nothing. No sounds, no movement, nothing except the occasional whistle of the wind through the bare treetops. I checked my watch, waited two more minutes, checked it again and then muttered, "Fuck it."

The main entrance of the warehouse was unlocked, as always. I remembered a bare light bulb that hung from the ceiling just to the right of the door, and I reached around for it in the dark before batting it and then grabbing the bulb on the rebound. I held it with one hand and located the little chain on the fixture, and I gave it a tug.

My eyes adjusted quickly. It only took a second, maybe a blink, for what I was seeing to register. Hyman Pietroski — nervous, solid, Auschwitz survivor Hyman Pietroski — was naked and hanging by a rope from an overhead beam. His head was at a preposterous angle to the rest of his body, the neck obviously broken, the skin of his face blue. His bowels had emptied on the warehouse floor beneath his feet. A kicked-over chair lay on its side.

All I could feel was my heart. All I could hear was the wind outside.

I walked the 20 feet or so from the entrance toward Hyman, forcing every step. As I got closer, I could see that his body had been battered. His back was facing me and it was bruised, and there was a welt on his left shoulder. I looked down from that shoulder and saw that his left pinky had been lopped off. But when I looked down, I didn't see it in the nasty puddle on the dirt floor — not that I searched very hard.

I walked around Hyman's body and viewed it from the front. I looked up at his chest and saw burn marks on both of his nipples. Black scorches on pink flesh. There was the stench from his bowels, but I also had myself convinced that I could smell burning hair. It was probably my imagination, but still.

Black scorches on pink flesh. Panicked, I automatically looked around the room, searching for the people who had done this as well as for the battery or the wires. But I couldn't find them — not the men, not the electrical gear. I think I must have relaxed for a second, and that's when it hit me, when I turned away and threw up, making my own mess on the floor, another site of fetid mud.

Tortured. That was the first thing I thought.

My fault. That was the next thing, the lasting thing.

4

I had, in fact, just kicked over my second bucket of Champagne that night, and Alfred had warned me, "The third one comes out of your check, and I'm not kidding." I was wiping up the last of it when a voice from the bar said, "Barkeep, a proper drink for a thirsty traveler, if you please."

"One Rhine Cocktail, coming up."

"Not even as a joke."

"I know, old man, I know."

It was Fritz, my boss at the Gehlen Organization. I had almost forgotten. Every three months, first Friday of the month, he made the trip up from Vienna.

"So, how's the Baltic workers' paradise treating you?"

"I tend bar."

"In the Baltic workers' paradise. You earn two salaries for, well, for what exactly?"

"Just drink," I said. I had begun mixing two Manhattans as soon as I heard his voice and pushed one of them across the bar. The other was for me.

"To Otto," Fritz said.

"Uncle Otto," I said.

"And who's paying for these?"

"Nobody, unless the boss comes out. Then you are."

"Said the man with two salaries."

Fritz was an old friend/running buddy of my Uncle Otto. Just before the war, a Gestapo captain killed Otto and threw him in the Rhine because he believed my uncle was conspiring with Fritz, a rival in the Abwehr. He wasn't, though. Fritz and Otto were just friends. And in the 20-odd years since, Fritz used me sometimes, and saved my ass other times, and became a kind of surrogate uncle. He also was my handler with Gehlen, a spy organization largely funded by the Americans and made up mostly of former German military men who had eastern-facing connections that the Americans couldn't match. Gehlen was the big boss.

We finished the first drinks and I made another round, and Fritz asked me, "So how is..."

Pause.

"...your sabbatical?"

He always asked it the same way — same pause, same words. Your sabbatical.

After Krakow, I needed some time. I just couldn't face... anything — and for some reason, that included Vienna. I had one friend there — Leon — but I had no real job and no one else, nothing except a well-filled bank account. And I just, well, I don't know. I drank to excess every day and then ate lunch. I didn't know what to do. I couldn't face home and I couldn't even contemplate being embedded in another country for months on end, with all of the pressure, just constant stress. So, Fritz came up with this idea. My sabbatical.

He arranged for the bartending job in Heringsdorf, a place I had never heard of, and all of the paperwork that would be required. It was open-ended, as long as I needed. There was only one catch. One day a month, I would still be a spy. That one day,

I would slip into Poland. We were right on the border — Ahlbeck and my apartment weren't much more than a mile from it. On the other side of some woods that had grown up over the dune was Swinoujscie, the first Polish town. And in Swinoujscie was a Catholic priest in a little parish who was doing a little observational work for the Gehlen Org between saying his rosary. Joyful Mystery, Sorrowful Mystery, Glorious Mystery, Luminous Mystery, Commie Spy Mystery — that's how it went for this guy.

Swinoujscie was a port, and what the priest did was observe stuff happening around the harbor pertaining to the Soviet presence: ships in and out, gun emplacements, stuff like that that. I would visit him and he would tell me, and then I would tell a Gehlen man — a big oaf named Gluck — who visited my bar. One day a month — no weapons, not particularly dangerous, not even overnight sometimes. For someone with my skillset, it really was pretty easy.

I was about to say something when I heard Alfred behind me, refilling his glass with club soda. I turned and saw him looking at the two half-drunk Manhattans on the bar. From there, his eyes raised to meet mine before he walked away. I knew he was going to look over his shoulder, though, so I made sure to be making out the receipt when he turned.

"Bad luck for you, but I'll only get you for two, not four," I said.

"And your boss will check?"

"Before he goes to sleep," I said.

Fritz just shook his head. Then I remembered and told him the story of Grundmann from Dresden, and the walk up the stairs to follow Ricky to the room on the second floor.

"Grundmann from Dresden, Grundmann from Dresden," Fritz said, repeating it a total of four times as a way of imprinting the name in his memory.

"Think it'll be worth anything?"

"Never know."

"So, a freebie for you, then. On the house."

"I'd rather have a free drink," Fritz said.

"No free drinks. Times are tough."

"I can't believe they haven't taken this place yet."

Heringsdorf was full of private villas that the East German government had already scooped up. Some of the hotels, too. But this wasn't like Berlin or the other big cities, where the Communist government had pretty efficiently taken over most private businesses — or, for sure, at least the bigger industries. Heringsdorf, even though it wasn't that far from Berlin — maybe four hours on a slow train — still had a kind of boondocks feel to it. Change was slower there.

"Most of the hotels are still privately held," I said. "But the Russians took some already, for hospitals and sanitariums and shit, and they've gone straight to the government."

"But, for how long..."

"Until they take The Denkler? Alfred says two, three years, and he'll be done — but he's determined to squeeze the last drop of juice out of the lemon before then. Wait, watch over my back."

I mixed two more Manhattans in record time and put the empties in the sink. I looked at Fritz and he gave me the thumbs up. He said the door to the office never opened.

"Six for the price of two — not bad, old man," I said.

"Still, the two..."

These visits really did tend to be more social than business. Fritz retold a couple of the old Otto stories, and I laughed in all the right places, and we nursed the third drink. And then he took a deep breath and performed the one bit of business ritual that he felt was required. Every three months, he asked if I was ready to come back full-time. He always said, "to come back to work."

"I am working."

"You're taking the kaiser's holiday."

"It's work."

"Fine, fine. I told you no pressure and I mean it. No pressure. I promise. A lot of days, in fact, it's the opposite."

"Meaning what?" I said.

"Meaning, a lot of days, I hope you never come back, not all the way back. That you find a life outside of... this."

"Getting sentimental in your old age?"

"Fuck you," he said, barely above a whisper. Then he caught my eyes and said, "We both know this is no life. I mean, I had a wife. I had a normal army career. Then Hitler and, well, shit. But I did have a life. I have those memories. But, well, you're not a kid anymore. I'll always think of you as Otto's nephew, but not a kid. Not anymore. And you have..."

He didn't finish the thought. He didn't need to. It was a thought I had every day, almost without fail — the thought that the life I had chosen had left me personally bankrupt. And now, with a mindless job, with Karin and Lotte... maybe? Hell, I had no idea. Maybe. But I really did have no idea.

"But you're still going to ask?" I said.

"Every three months," Fritz said. "First Friday of the month."

5

The Barge was the bar in Ahlbeck where most of the hotel employees drank after we wrapped up work. It was a 20-minute walk, give or take, from The Denkler and just a few blocks from my apartment.

It was, I imagined, like every late-night bar that catered to service workers. That is, it was a semi-dump. In The Barge's case, the primary feature was that the closer you got to the bar itself, the more your shoes stuck to the floor. The only amenity worth talking about was the closing time. Last call came at 3:30 a.m., and the shooing out the door stage began at 3:45, and if you weren't out by 4, shooing became shoving. The night bartender/owner/bouncer did the shooing and the shoving. A massive man, he was known universally as Tiny.

I arrived at 12:30 that night with the intention of having one. But one became three when Gus Braun strode in and bellowed, "Tiny, I love what you've done with the place." It's what he said every time he came into The Barge. That night, Tiny never even looked up from the beer tap he was fiddling with.

Gus was the head waiter at The Denkler's second-best restaurant — which made him, as he said, "The king of the fucking lunch rush." Every time we had a drink, or three, there was at least a 15-minute interlude in the conversation when he complained about his lot in life.

"'Here's the extra mayonnaise you asked for, madam,'" he said, putting on his obsequious waiter voice.

"All work is honorable," I said.

"'Sir, could you please ask your son to stop throwing rolls around the dining room?'"

"You could just quit."

"And do what?" Gus said. "Being a head waiter is all that I know."

He had been at The Denkler for nearly three years, longer than me. He didn't talk much about the journey, except for the basics. He had been reluctant to offer any details at all the first few times we talked, dismissing my questions with a wave and a weary, "I'm just one of the travelers."

Little by little over the months, he provided the outline. He had lived in Swinoujscie during the war, except it wasn't Swinoujscie then. It was Swinemünde, a very German city — German forever — that was very much on the German side of the Germany-Poland border. But after they finally blew the full-time whistle on Hitler, well, to the victors went the spoils — and they were determined to spoil the lives of Gus Braun and a couple of million other people who had been German their entire lives.

What happened was, if you looked at a map of Poland, the Soviets decided that they wanted a piece from the right side of the country for themselves. Problem was, it was full of Poles. The solution was to add a new slice of Poland to the left side of the map, the side that bordered with Germany, and to ship a bunch of those Poles from the right slice to the left slice. Oh, and to put a couple of million German citizens from the left slice onto trains and trucks and donkey carts and drop them, well, where? With no compensation for their homes and farms and whatever they left behind, those millions of Germans mostly ended up in Hamburg and thereabouts.

"No jobs, no homes, the clothes on our backs. Welcome!" Gus said. The way he told the story, he gave Hamburg a year.

"Fucking filthy place, and bombed to shit besides," was his description. "People were eating rats, sleeping rough. If a woman under the age of 40 wasn't whoring herself out to the British soldiers, she and her kids were starving — and that was even if she had a husband. Just think about that for a second. You're a man, and you survived the war, and the only way you can survive the post-war, the only way you can feed your family, is if you allow your wife to..."

He stopped, took a breath.

"If I was one of those husbands, poor bastards, I might have just hanged myself."

Another pause. Another breath.

"It was just hell, just an unending nightmare."

"Hitler, the gift who keeps on giving," I said.

"Yeah, maybe. But you can't tell me the rest of the Allies couldn't have told Uncle Joe to keep the German border where it was. No, this one is on them."

"But if it hadn't have been..."

"No, this one is on them," Gus said. He had this tone sometimes, the one that ended conversations, and he used it there.

Anyway, Swinemünde became Swinoujscie, Stettin became Szczecin, and a few hundred smaller German places became a few hundred more unpronounceable Polish places — and Gus tried to make it in Hamburg until he said he couldn't anymore. At which point, he made the decision to leave the British sector and resettle in East Germany.

"I still can't believe it," I said.

"Can't believe what?"

"That you came back."

"It's what I know."

"Communism?"

"The beach, asshole. This beach. The Baltic. The sand. The air."

"Hamburg has the Baltic. Hamburg has air."

"Not the same," Gus said, half to himself. "It's not the same. Besides, nothing's stopping you from leaving and you're still here. You could get on the train to East Berlin tomorrow, and hop on the U-Bahn, and get off at one of the stations in West Berlin, and voilà. But you're still here."

"I'm too lazy for all of that," I said.

"I bet," Gus said.

It had been well-established that both of us had a backstory and neither of us was interested in telling it. So, a truce. Mostly, we got drunk and gossiped about the people we worked with — who was screwing who, and who was managing to steal the most when Alfred wasn't looking, and how exactly we might hasten the demise of the head waiter in the main dining room, 70-year-old Gerhard Lutz.

"You put something in his sherry and I get his job," Gus said.

"I steal the odd free drink. I do not commit murder."

"It's not murder. It's a mercy killing."

"Mercy for you, the king of the fucking lunch rush."

"Mercy is mercy," Gus said, at which point he began laughing and telling the story of the 19-year-old busboy, the 17-year-old waitress, and the time Gerhard Lutz found them in the midst of some extracurricular activity behind a stack of canned food crates in the pantry.

"That was a two-sherry night for the old boy," Gus said. "That was the night I should have done it. Nobody would have doubted a heart attack that night."

That was our general level of friendship. Still, I occasionally probed.

"I bet you felt like you were going against traffic when you came back."

"The wrong way on a one-way street? Yeah," Gus said. "Even the East German border guards were surprised. They didn't even have the right forms — you know, for somebody trying to get in."

6

There was a choice — walk along the beach or walk along the promenade. The way I made the decision was mostly about the moon. On a black night, I tended to walk along the beach. When the moon was fuller, I tended to walk along the promenade because the canopy of trees provided a cosset of darkness.

It wasn't much more than a mile from Ahlbeck to the Polish border. That night, I covered about three-quarters of the distance on the beach. It was a warm night, even at 3 a.m., a calm night, and I actually enjoyed myself, comforted by the sound of the gently crashing Baltic waves.

For whatever reason, these excursions never really worried me — not to the point where I got careless, but still. I mean, I knew the reason. As Fritz liked to tell me, "You've seen some shit," and, well, this wasn't that. After the first time, I knew exactly what I would be up against — and it wasn't much.

About a quarter-mile from the border, I made my way from the shoreline and up into the tree-covered dune. Here was the setup: a beach that was maybe 300 feet wide, then about 50 feet of sandy dune, then maybe another 300 feet of tree-covered dune, then the promenade.

There were some paths through the trees, but they tended to be narrow and overgrown and hard to identify in the dark. It made for a slow, difficult slog. I wore gloves and kept my hands out in front of me, which helped me to navigate among the obstacles without ripping up my skin. A couple of months earlier, I had forgotten the gloves and had to make up some bullshit story for Karin about helping a gardener at The Denkler haul away some bushes he had pruned down to the stumps. I think she believed me.

The day before the monthly venture, Karin and I had a variation on the same conversation.

"Tell me again what takes two days?"

"It's how long it takes."

"You're only going to Berlin and loading up a truck and bringing it back. That's 10 or 12 hours with a long lunch thrown in. So what takes two days?"

"Incompetence takes two days," I would say.

The way my story went, the two days were spent on The Denkler's monthly liquor run to the warehouse in Berlin. And the truth was, The Denkler did make a monthly liquor run to the warehouse in Berlin. Only, I wasn't involved. Alfred made the trip himself along with his son/driver/loader/unloader. Alfred's job was to carry the bribe money. Because in the workers' paradise, the only way for a humble hotel owner in Heringsdorf to get his hands on English gin, French Champagne and the like was to pay out the ass to whatever party official was in charge of liquor imports. Hence, the briefcase that Alfred actually cuffed to his wrist for the journey to Berlin, like a guy in a spy movie.

"Why you?" Karin asked.

"Why me what?"

"Why do you make the liquor run?"

"Apparently, I'm trustworthy," I said.

Even if the trips to Swinoujscie didn't take even 18 hours — I would be back the next evening, soon after dusk — I always told her it would be two days, just in case. And she seemed to buy it, even if she pouted.

I thought of Karin, and those conversations, as I pulled on the gloves and entered the trees. The border itself was somewhere in the middle of the woods. Both the East Germans and the Poles had border guards on either side — two of each on the promenade, two of each on the beach, each pair behind its own gate. What became obvious the first time I made the crossing was that while the East German guards were lazy, sticking to their posts, the Polish guards occasionally waded into the woods. They didn't stay long, and they weren't particularly stealthy — they traveled in pairs, sneaked cigarettes, chatted the whole time, and maybe stayed for five minutes — but it was something to think about. In reality, it was the only worry.

Generally, the toughest part was calculating when to emerge from the woods and onto the promenade on the Polish side. Because of the contours of the road, the guards at the border couldn't see more than about 500 feet into Polish territory. There had been no guards in the woods that night, and I guess I got lazy. When I poked my head out of the trees, I was only about 250 feet from the guards. I saw them but I was certain they hadn't seen me. And then I heard the barking.

Dogs. This was a new wrinkle, and one that scared the hell out of me. I scampered back into the woods as the barking got louder. I listened — it wasn't dogs, but a single dog. And as I hid behind a tree in a nasty, wet depression in the ground, I could tell a couple of things. One, that the dog was on a lead. And, two, that the guards couldn't be bothered.

"It's just a goddamned rabbit," the one guard said.

"Maybe."

"He barks three times a night. Every night for the last two weeks. Forty, fifty barks. And have we ever found anybody?"

"Maybe we need to look harder."

"Fuck that. Here."

I could smell cigarette smoke. They were probably a hundred feet away. Why wasn't the dog going crazy? Probably the cigarette smoke masked my scent. Anyway, I wasn't sure what the "here" meant when the guard said it, but I could guess.

"You make that in your bathtub?"

"Old family recipe."

"Rancid potatoes and dirty socks?"

"Fresh potatoes and a loving time-honored technique. But if you're not interested…"

"Hand it back here," the guard said. Drinking, smoking, distracted, uncaring. They were the working definition of every soldier in every army I had ever encountered — that is, when the duty was shit and when their superior officers were nowhere to be seen.

Gradually, the sound of the footfalls and the smell of the cigarette smoke faded. It was only after I stood up that I realized it would be hours before my pants fully dried.

7

That day, as on most of my trips, I needed to kill about two and a half hours before I went to the church. It wasn't hard. By 5 a.m. the streets of Swinoujscie weren't busy but they weren't deserted either — and that worked fine for my purposes. In a port town, there always seemed to be men coming and going at all hours from docks and ships and shipyards. Along with them, 5 a.m. brought the old men and their dogs, or the old couples stretching their legs and maybe seeing the sunrise on the beach. I fit right in — walking some, parking myself on a bench some. In all of my trips, I had never seen a cop stop anybody for any reason.

At 6 a.m., I began walking from the beach to the church. Stella Maris. Star of the Sea. It was a little red brick building on a side street about 15 minutes from the beach. Maybe less.

The street that it was on, Piastowska, was the middle of an oasis amid a desert of rubble. At the end of the war, the Allies bombed the hell out of Swinoujscie, which was then still Swinemünde, and still very much a German port. The way the story went, with the Soviets coming from the east, the United Kingdom and the United States wanted to make sure that Uncle

Joe didn't get his hands on all of the German ships and armaments, so they concocted a military reason to blow the place to hell. The story might be bullshit but I always thought it rang true.

Anyway, probably half of the town was flattened in the process, and probably 25 percent of it was still in piles more than five years later. But there Stella Maris was, untouched. Two blocks in any direction were mountains of bricks with weeds growing out of the crevices, but the church sat there, pristine.

Why does a building survive while others don't? I asked myself every time I made the walk. Why? Because the kid who pushed the button in the bomber was delayed by a sneeze, or a crackle in his radio, or just slow reflexes? A sneeze being the difference between a leveled row of buildings on one street and an untouched brick church two streets farther south?

I entered the church and took a seat in the back row. The 6 a.m. Mass was winding down, Communion time. There were about 20 people in the seats, mostly old biddies with scarves knotted under their chins but also a couple of men from the shipyard in their work clothes and with their lunch pails perched next to them in the pews.

The Mass ended and the priest exited through a door to the right of the altar. Maybe two minutes later, he came back through the same door, minus the green vestments. Instead, he wore a black cassock and a purple thing around his neck that he called a stole.

At the back of the church, on the left side, was a confessional. It was the kind I hated in that it was completely open. The priest sat in the middle, in a booth of sorts with two screened openings on either side. There were kneelers opposite the screens, and the priest would turn from his left to his right, open the screen, and hear the person's confession. I hated that you weren't behind a curtain when you knelt there, as in most of the churches I had seen. But it was what it was.

I had done this confessional bit before with a priest contact. Twice, I thought, but damned if I could remember the details. I was pretty sure I did it in Cologne, in the cathedral, but the other place, I just wasn't sure. Maybe Limoges. Or... nah. I just couldn't think.

But, I mean, how screwed up was my life that I couldn't remember? These were life-and-death moments when they were happening — or at least potentially life-and-death. But now, they were just... gone. Pfft. Life. Death. Whatever.

Two biddies had scurried over and got in position as soon as Mass ended. I sat in my seat and watched them confess from about 30 feet away. They looked like the kind that never missed a week, and each took maybe three minutes. If either of them had done anything worse than say "damn" when she burned her hand on a saucepan, I would have been shocked.

I waited for them to finish saying their penance at the altar rail, and for a third stray old lady who had lit a candle in front of the Blessed Mother statue. When the church was empty, I waited another two minutes and then I walked over to the confessional and knelt down.

The screen opened.

"About fucking time..."

"Said the man of God."

"You know what I mean."

"Yeah," I said. I did know what he meant. Every minute we spent together was another minute he was at risk.

Father Piotr Sciabotski. Pete. Late thirties, early forties, good head of hair, and a true believer. With the pleasantries complete, he rattled off the stuff he had seen — the big shift change at the shipyard taking place at 11 p.m. now instead of midnight; the arrival of a massive but rusty old destroyer with the word

"Vanya" stenciled on its bow; a new series of searchlights being installed in a marshy area to the east of the town. Standard shit, it seemed, none of it particularly meaningful by itself.

"Kind of a yawn," Pete said.

"Yeah maybe. But we don't know how the pieces fit. We're not privy to..."

"To the fucking mosaic. Yeah, yeah, I heard you the last five times."

"You sure say 'fuck' a lot. You know, for a priest."

"It's the company I keep," he said. "But seriously, I feel like I'm taking a pretty big risk here for... well, for what?"

"The mosaic, Petey."

"My father called me Petey."

"And how did that go?"

"Hated it, hated him," the priest said. Then, he sighed. "God, I feel worn out."

This had been building, this "worn out" complaint. It was always vague, though, never more than a generalization, and I didn't pry. I did ask if he had been stopped by a cop or felt as if he was being followed, but that was it. When he told me that it was none of that, that there had been no tangible sign that he was in any kind of danger, I let him be.

I mean, spies all had stress. It was the primary occupational hazard. Spies all drank themselves to sleep when they weren't pursuing meaningless sex. And I just figured that was true even if the spy was a priest, and that he had access to the liquor cabinet in the rectory — and probably the girls who cooked the meals, too, if he was so inclined. His stress, his problems. All I could do was try to calm him with bullshit visions of the mosaic. I mean, I had my own problems.

"How's your pastor?" I said, changing the subject. "Any better?"

"Oh, man," Pete said. He looked over his shoulder at the

empty church and checked his wristwatch. We had talked about Monsignor Bosko before. Pete said his boss was 68 years old, drinking excessively, functional pretty much between 10 a.m. and 2 p.m. — "and not a minute past two." After that, the Monsignor was useless for the rest of the day.

"But it's not just that," he said. "Like, he's becoming forgetful. And, like, I'm not sure he has control over all of his impulses anymore. I mean, I came upon him the other day and he had unbuttoned his cassock and was taking a piss in one of the potted plants in the sitting room of the rectory. And, like, he was naked under the cassock."

"You mean, you wear pants?"

"Fuck you. At least underpants."

"That's rough. But, I mean, he isn't the first priest to get old. They must have a plan to deal with that. Do his bosses know?"

"That's the problem — we don't really have bosses these days. I mean, we do — there's a bishop near Szczecin. But even though they moved the border, and even though we're in Poland, and even though all of the German priests in all of the parishes got their asses shipped out with everybody else, we're still under the control of the archbishop in Berlin. The pope seems to think this moving the border business is just a temporary inconvenience and that it's all going back the way it was someday soon."

"Tell that to the two million people who got kicked out and the two million who jumped into their beds."

"Might be three million," Pete said. "Unofficial church survey. Or maybe they're just guessing. So, anyway the archbishop in Berlin, he sends his guy to Szczecin, his auxiliary bishop, but I'm not sure exactly what he does. He's in charge, kind of, but we never see him. Like, never. I don't know what the man looks like except for a blurry newspaper photo. He was bald but you couldn't make out any of his features."

"So, like a penis," I said, helpfully. Peter laughed.

"But the thing is, even if he did get a look at the Monsignor, I mean, I don't even know how the bishop communicates with Berlin. It's not like he can just pick up the phone."

He looked up at his watch again.

"Go say a Hail Mary at the altar rail," the priest said. "I've got breakfast with the old man and a stack of Confirmation certificates for him to sign before 2 o'clock rolls around."

8

You work odd hours, you make odd acquaintances. One of mine was Gerd Fromm, who owned a fishing boat that called a cove in Ahlbeck home. The fishing beach was near the big old pier that jutted hundreds of feet out into the Baltic. I had met Gerd on a walk one morning, and we took to chatting while he repaired his nets. He worked early, I worked late, and we intersected at about 11 a.m. He told me stories about the sea, I told him stories about the drunks, and we occasionally shared a nip from a bottle he kept in an ice chest. Vodka, neat.

As he said, "Alcohol, so versatile. Helps you rev up, helps me wind down."

One time, our stories intersected. I was telling him about this customer at the bar, a particularly annoying guy wearing a sport coat that was just this side of yellow, when Gerd stopped me.

"Banana Sam!" he said.

"What?"

"Banana Sam."

"Because of the jacket?"

"Not exactly," Gerd said. "He used to have a boat. Sold it a couple of years ago after he came into a little money — it's a shit life on the boats."

"Come on, you love it."

"I don't love it. I just don't know any different."

"Anyway, Banana Sam?"

"He was known for two things when he had a boat. He caught less than anybody else, and he spent two nights a week working hard to get laid."

"In the yellow sport coat?"

Gerd nodded.

"And how did he do?"

"Caught more than he did on the sea, surprisingly enough. But he always brought them back to the boat — which, less surprisingly, had a devastating effect on his repeat business. So it was always one-and-done. And there was this one night when he was moored right next to me, and he had drunk a lot, and his catch that night was particular loud, and the wind was blowing in my direction, and her voice carried, and at one point she yelled, "Goddammit Sam, it's softer than a month-old banana."

"Ah," I said. "Banana Sam."

"And the yellow jacket was just too perfect," he said. "I call him 'Banana Sam' every time I see him, and he has no idea that I heard."

Gerd sold herring sandwiches off the back of his boat. They were really good, too, the sandwiches — fresh fish caught that morning, grilled and slathered with something on a roll. He had a loyal clientele of people who lived nearby and worked in the guesthouses along the promenade. You knew he was open for business because you smelled the grill if you were close enough or because you saw the red flag he flew from the pole on the bow of the boat.

Lotte loved the place, and Karin and I would take her every

couple of weeks. And every time we showed up, Gerd gave me a look that he then punctuated it with the same four words once it was just me and him.

Four words: "Don't fuck this up."

That day, Gerd took Lotte up onto the boat to show her where he slept and to allow her to help him make the sandwiches. Karin and I were going for a walk on the pier.

"Bring me an ice cream on the way back? Pleeeeease!"

"Only if you're good," Karin said.

"I'm always good," Lotte said.

Pause.

"But how will you even know if I've been good when you're gone because you won't be here with me to see?" she said.

"Smart girl," Gerd said.

"Too smart," Karin said.

The ice cream was sold inside the small building at the beginning of the pier, the one with the four turrets on top. We would buy it on the way back. It was a pretty calm day but, even at that, the wind whipped as you got several feet out into the Baltic. By about November, it would be too cold to even think about a walk much past the small building.

I put my arm around Karin, and she snuggled in a little closer as we walked, using my body to shield her from the worst of the wind.

"You know, I'm worried about you," she said.

"I'm sleeping fine."

"You're a bad liar. And you forget that we share a bed sometimes."

"Did you ever think it's you that keeps me awake?"

"I'm serious."

"I know you are."

Karin knew about my past, what I did for a living. I decided, soon after I met her, that complete honesty was going to be required if this was to have a chance. I made a pretty quick exception to the honesty rule — she didn't know about my monthly visit to Father Piotr Sciabotski — but that was it. Anything else, if she asked, I told her. That included the night I found Hyman Pietroski hanging in the abandoned warehouse in Krakow.

"You really think that's the whole reason?" she said.

"I know it is."

"Maybe a doctor..."

"No doctors," I said. But that was really the only time I shut her down, when she suggested a psychologist. The rest of the time, I listened and answered and gave ground when she seemed to be making sense. And other than the doctor thing, the only nerve she really struck was the one where the past and the future collided.

As in:

"But how do you know?"

"Because I do. I know. I'm positive. I'm out of the business."

"But how can you be sure?"

"Because I am sure. I'm a bartender. In Ahlbeck. With a girl-friend and her daughter and a nice, dull life."

"And you're sure that isn't the reason why you can't sleep?" she said that day as we walked on the pier, just as she had said it a dozen other times over the months.

It had never even occurred to me that she might be right, and I really didn't believe she was. The sleeping bit had started well before I met her. I knew it was because of Hyman, and the guilt I felt about Hyman, and probably the accumulation of shit over the years. It wasn't because I missed living under an assumed identity in a new city. It wasn't because I missed the smell of a pistol I had just fired at a person I didn't know.

Time would heal me. It was just taking a little longer this time, but time would be the answer. A doctor might speed the process —Karin was right — but that was out. I couldn't trust an East German shrink any more than I could trust a Stasi captain. They all reported up the chain — I felt confident about that — and I just couldn't even contemplate the risk. And the idea of leaving The Denkler and Karin and Lotte for weeks or months of therapy in West Germany or Vienna — that was out, too. That was something else I didn't want to contemplate.

So, time. But over the months, Karin couldn't hide her concerns. And that day on the pier, those concerns were more pointed than they had ever been.

She said, "If you can't shake this, if you can't get out of your business and stay out of your business..."

"I am out of my business," I said. Again, lying.

"...If you can't stay out, then we can't keep doing this. I won't do it to myself. I especially won't do it to Lotte. She likes you too much already. I can't have her falling completely in love with a man who is going to disappear into some..."

"I'm not going to disappear," I said, and then the two of us went quiet. We were at the end of the pier, and we said nothing to each other as we walked back.

"Just her?" I said, finally. We were approaching the little building where they sold the ice cream.

"Just her what?"

"Just Lotte? Is she the only thing you're worried about?"

"Not just her — especially her," Karin said. "I'm a grown woman. I've seen shit. I've lost a husband. I've raised a daughter on my own. I'm tougher than I look. It would hurt but I would survive. But Lotte... no. If you can't stay out of this, this, this whatever, this business, then...."

"I'm out," I said, quietly. Lying again.

She went silent for the second time after that. Lotte

screamed for joy a few minutes later when we brought her the ice cream, and we all laughed when she ended up wearing as much of the chocolate as she consumed. But I could see from the look on Gerd's face that he could sense the tension between Karin and me.

9

The next month, my visit to see Father Pete was so uneventful as to be a complete waste of time. It was a rainy night when I crossed the border, and rainy nights were the easiest nights because the guards never left their little shacks on either side of the border, both beach and promenade. I could have pranced through the woods bellowing an aria and none of them would have heard me.

When I got to the confessional, Pete was nervous again. Just anxious about everything and nothing. I asked him if it was anything specific, and he said it wasn't, and I didn't know what to do.

"You want to go for a drink or something?"

"It's six-fucking-thirty."

"Desperate times."

"Not that desperate," the priest said.

The sum total of his surveillance information that month consisted of his confirmation that the shift change from midnight to 11 p.m. at the shipyard seemed permanent. I did my best to hide just how worthless that tidbit was, but he knew.

"I'm sorry. I mean, you risk your life every time you cross that border, and for me to have such weak shit in return…"

"I'm not risking my life, trust me," I said.

"But what if you got caught?"

"That's when I would tell the border guards about the voluptuous 30-year-old I was screwing in Swinoujscie and throw myself on the mercy of their hormones."

"I don't know."

"I'm 75 percent sure it would work. They're probably kids, early twenties. I'm sure they spend their whole shift every night comparing and lying about their experiences with voluptuousness."

"And the other 25 percent?"

"They might arrest me," I said. "In no case would they shoot me."

The priest leaned back in his chair, sighed, ran the fingers of both hands through his hair, and sighed again. Then he stole a look over his shoulder and confirmed that we were the only two in the church.

"Maybe I just need to talk to Father—"

He stopped.

"Oh, shit — I almost told you his name."

"Father X. Your, what, controller?"

"I don't know what you call him," Pete said. "Controller. I guess. He gives me instructions, pep talks, whatever."

"He's in Krakow, right?"

"Yeah. I see him four times a year. I always time it to coincide with a visit to my old uncle. Great uncle — is it great uncle or grand uncle? My grandfather's brother. He's, like, 92. Anyway, that's the excuse I use for going home to Krakow. And that's when I have my meeting with Father X. January, April, July, October. Always on the fifth. Always The Steam Whistle café across from the station. Always 5 p.m. Always 5 p.m. on the fifth."

"And what does he tell you?"

"My great uncle? Usually about his bowel movements, or lack thereof."

"Charming," I said.

"Father X? He recruited me, he convinced me how important it was. I guess he mostly just tells me that there is a network in place, and that I'm not alone in this. I guess that makes me feel better, hearing it every once in a while from another human being rather than just telling it to myself."

"And what do you tell him about me?" I said.

"Conceited much?"

"Come on."

"I tell him that you're an agnostic asshole, but that I enjoy a challenge."

"And..."

"And Father X said, and I will quote him directly here, 'Your job is not to save his soul, it's to save our own ass.'"

"Smart man, that Father X," I said.

10

Weeks later, as summer melted into fall, I spent more time on the beach. In my mind, it was the best time of the year on the Baltic. It could be gone in a blink some years, the time between the hot summer sun and, well, cold as balls, but it was the best little slice. The tourists were mostly gone, the beaches quiet. I went out of my way to enjoy it, and that included the night Gus Braun and I lifted a bottle of rye from the cellar at The Denkler and took the long walk on the sand from Heringsdorf to Ahlbeck and then toward the Polish border.

It was a bright night, the moon nearly full. It was chilly but not cold, and the rye we passed back and forth filled in whatever deficiencies our jackets might have manifested.

"It's not The Barge," I said, waving my arm in the direction of the Baltic, its waters barely moving in the moonlight.

"Thank God," Gus said. "I can't tell you how much I love it."

We had no intention of going all the way to the border — at least, I knew I didn't — even though walking on the beach at night was perfectly legal, even with an open bottle. We got within a hundred yards or so, and that was close enough. In the moonlight, you could see the short fence that ran up from the dune to the waterline — and even a few yards into the water. You could also see the two little guard shacks, one on either side of the fence.

I looked up toward the dune for some reason and saw, well, nothing. It took a few seconds for the nothingness to register, though — I actually did a double-take. The trees on either side of the fence were gone. Well, about 10 yards were gone. Those were the trees I sneaked through in order to cross the border on my visits to and from Swinoujscie.

"What's that?" I said.

"Death strip."

"Death what?"

"Death strip," Gus said. "It's a spot where they can see who might be trying to sneak across the border."

"Who would want to sneak?" I said. "Aren't these two countries friends? Poland and East Germany, together as Communist brothers, united in their enjoyment of the smell of Stalin's farts?"

"Friends, maybe," Gus said. "But friends in the same way that co-workers aiming at the same promotion are friends. They never take an eye off of us, and we never take an eye off of them. Maybe someday, when all of us are comfortable in our socialist fellowship, it'll be different. Not now, though. In the here and now, it's all smiles and side-eyes."

Death strip. Christ. The idea of dogs and guards was bad enough. The border being completely denuded of trees would make it impossible. Even if it was just a term of art — death strip — this new border arrangement might put me out of business. That might not be the worst thing, either.

"When did they start?"

"I walked down here last week, and they were just beginning," Gus said. "One of the guards told me that's what they called it — death strip. He said it might take seven weeks to finish. So, six more. Something like that. Six, seven."

My mind wandered around the possibilities but only for a few seconds. Then it was Gus's turn to wave his arm at the vista — not at the Baltic this time, but due east.

In the distance, in the moonlight, you could see the taller bits of Swinoujscie. It wasn't two miles from the border. You could see the black silhouettes even at night — a couple of ship building structures, the lighthouse, a couple of taller buildings.

"The one on the right — that's The Potsdamer," Gus said.

"Your old place?"

He nodded.

"I wonder what they call it now?" he said.

"Maybe the same."

"No chance," Gus said.

I actually knew what they called it now: The Swinoujscie Inn. I walked by it every time on the way to Stella Maris. Of course, I couldn't tell Gus that.

"Nicer than The Denkler?" I said.

He spat on the sand.

"The Potsdamer was a palace. The table linens — you've never seen white so white. They blinded you. And they had two women working full-time just to iron the table cloths and the napkins. And another girl, whose whole job — eight hours a day — was just to fold the napkins into these things that looked like tents. Eight hours! Crisp, white — blinding. The Denkler is a shithole by comparison."

"That's hard to believe."

"A shithole," Gus said. "I mean, even the rye is barely worth stealing."

I nearly snorted what was in my mouth through my nose.

"You know, Swinemünde was the kaiser's beach before this place," he said.

"Just because it's older doesn't make it better. I mean, come on. The kaiser took tea at The Denkler."

"So they say."

"You doubt it?"

"If you believe the stories, the kaiser drank tea at every villa up and down Dunenstrasse, supposedly," Gus said. "And there's no way it's true. But at The Potsdamer, it's an established fact that we hosted the kaiser and the tsar for tea in 1905."

"Really? Not bullshit?"

"My grandfather was there. He served them. And he told my father, and my father described it to me a hundred times before he died."

"A hundred times? The same way every time?"

"Well, the story did kind of morph over the years," Gus said. "By the end, it wasn't tea, but vodka. And it wasn't sandwiches and cakes, but roast beef and pheasant. And it wasn't just the kaiser and the tsar, but two other unnamed lovelies joined them. That was how the old man was telling it a week before he died."

"No, you're right, no bullshit there," I said.

Gus smiled.

"It's a proven fact that the kaiser and tsar met in Swinemünde in 1905. As for the rest... I was head waiter in the best restaurant in The Potsdamer, not the fucking lunch room."

He stopped, spat again.

"I took over as head waiter from my father, and he took over from his father. So, let's just say the Braun family name is invested in the story of the kaiser and the tsar — whatever they consumed."

"Including the lovelies," I said.

"That was never stated."

"Only implied."

"A hell of an implication, that," Gus said.

We commandeered an extra-large strandkorb and fiddled

with the lock until the hasp fell out of the rotting wood. We turned it toward Swinoujscie, and sat on the bench, and continued working on the bottle of rye. It was when I passed it back to him that I noticed the tears on Gus's cheeks glistening in the moonlight. I tried to look away, but he saw that I had seen.

Another long pull on the rye bottle.

"I gotta tell you something," he said.

11

"The Polish special forces got to Swinemünde before the Russian army did," Gus said. He had wiped his face with his sleeve and he wasn't letting go of the bottle. He wasn't drinking it, either. He was just clutching it, tighter than he needed to. Strangling it.

"I mean, not that it mattered, I guess," he said. "They all worked for the same people in the end. But it was Polish. Polish special forces."

He stopped. Then he did drink some.

"It's funny — we actually did survive the bombing. Fucking Brits. Our house was completely intact. Really, our whole little neighborhood was untouched somehow. I have no idea how. All I know is, all we could talk about was how we were."

A crackle on the radio. A sneeze. Lucky.

Gus looked at me. He saw the question that I was afraid to ask. He just saw it in my eyes, I guess.

"Yes, we," he said, quietly. "Me, my wife, my daughter. Me, Connie and Gretch. Gretchen. Fifteen years old. You wouldn't have believed her smile. Light up the Olympic stadium in

Berlin. And always there. War years, teenage shit, didn't matter. It was never gone for long. God, that smile."

Gus started crying again and strangling the bottle again. He didn't try to hide the tears this time. He was not ashamed of them, not even a little, not after he had gotten started.

"You know, you don't have to," I said.

"No, I do have to. It's been five years and I've never told the story, not once. I need to tell someone."

"I'm honored," I said.

"You're available," he said.

"Asshole," I said.

"Asshole," he said, and then handed me the bottle. I took a long drink and then I handed it back. There was still probably a quarter of it left.

"It was a few weeks later," Gus said. "The town, I mean, it was in shock. A lot of people were just catatonic. Lost their homes. Lost everything. And then the Russians were coming. But the Polish special forces were ahead of them — I don't know, maybe a week ahead. And it started, well, almost right away."

I knew the stories about the Russian army, and what they stole, and how they raped women, all women, and girls, too. There was nothing subtle about it. It was brutal beyond words. And there Gus was, his tears glistening in the moonlight, trying to find them anyway. Trying to find the words.

"Polish security forces," he said. "They kicked in the door. It was two of them, both with rifles. The one of them clubbed me over the head with the butt of his rifle, knocked me out for a few minutes. When I woke up, I was tied to a chair — they'd yanked out the electrical cords from a couple of lamps."

He stopped and seemed to be having a conversation with himself. His lips weren't moving but it seemed to be a kind of internal monologue. I could only guess, but it was almost certainly revolving around two questions: "What could I have done differently?" and "What if?" After a few seconds, again without a word, Gus waved his hand helplessly in front of his face.

"Connie first, then Gretch," he said. "The bedroom door was closed, but I could tell by the screams. I don't have any pictures. I don't have shit, really, but the sound of those screams when I wake up in the middle of the night."

"Really, you don't..."

"I do," he said. "Just let me get through it. When the screaming stopped, and the bedroom door opened, this big redheaded guy was doing up his pants. Very distinctive name: Carney. I mean, not Polish — but he was in the uniform. Polish special forces.

"He was putting on his coat, and he saw me staring, and he said, 'What the fuck are you looking at?' In Polish, which I half understood.

"And then he said, 'Tasty.'"

I took the bottle. I needed the bottle.

"He went for the door and his partner said, 'What about him?' And the redheaded Carney, he said, 'They can untie him.' And then they left and slammed the door, and I shuffled the chair across the floor toward the bedroom, and the two of them were in there, Connie and Gretch, sitting on the floor, just holding onto each other and jammed into the far corner of the room."

Out of the corner of my eye, I someone approaching. It was one of the East German border guards. He saw us, and without a word I held out the bottle, and the kid took a drink and handed it back. He might have been 18.

"You can't sleep on the beach," he said.

"Understood," I said.

"Be gone in a half-hour," he said.

"Understood," I said.

He went back to his shack. Gus just kept staring past him, past him and over him, at the silhouette of Swinoujscie in the distance. But it would always be Swinemünde for him.

"They seemed okay — really, like, by the next morning," Gus said.

"I don't know what it was. Maybe like adrenaline or something — but they got back to it. But we never talked about it. I didn't know what to say, and they were handling it. They were fucking rocks, and I was so mad but I was also so amazed at, I don't know, their resilience. I mean, I didn't protect them, let them down—"

"The hell with that — there's nothing you could have done," I said.

"You weren't there."

"The guy knocked you out with his rifle and would have killed you with it the next time. There's nothing you could have done."

"I could have got killed," he said. A whisper.

Gus said he was called back to work the next week at The Potsdamer. The Russians were coming and the big brass was going to be using the hotel as its headquarters. He said work was busy, too, as the Soviet army chief arrived, and that he was glad for the distraction.

"The Russians drink late and they eat late, so we kept the restaurant open late," Gus said. "It was probably 2 a.m. when I got home. That's when I found them. They were sitting at the kitchen table, heads down on the kitchen table. I thought they were asleep until I saw the note. It was in Connie's writing, just one word. 'Sorry,' it said. There was a small tin of arsenic spilled over on the floor."

And then, it all came out. Gus sobbed so hard that he threw up in the sand, and then he sat a little more upright and I put my arm around him and he sunk his face into my chest and just cried like a baby. Five minutes is a long time, but that's how long he bawled. He went until there was nothing left. And then we stood up and started walking back to Ahlbeck.

I held out the bottle.

"Nah," he said, so I finished it and then tossed it as far as I could into the Baltic.

As we got to Ahlbeck and started toward out apartments, Gus stopped at a bench along the promenade and sat down. Between the moon and a streetlight, I got a good look at his face. It was a combination of exhausted and relaxed, if that makes any sense.

"Thank you," he said.

I waved my hand.

"No, thank you. It was good. You helped me. I hoped I puked some of it up back there, the shit I've been carrying."

"Well, it certainly smelled like shit," I said, and he laughed.

"We're never going to talk about this again," he said. "But there's one more thing I want to say. It's about the weather."

"The what?"

"The weather," he said. "On the day it happened, there wasn't a cloud in the sky that day. Führer weather — remember?"

Gus thought I was German. Never married. Too old for anything but the home guard in the second war. Pathetic loner. Bartender. Semi-alcoholic. Fin. Now he had told me his story but I was never going to tell him mine.

"Just a perfect day. And the sky — I actually looked up the color in a book in the library after I got to Hamburg. Cerulean blue. Well, I can't stand the color now. I can't stand days with no clouds. I force myself out most times, but a lot of my sick days at The Denkler — Führer weather. Cerulean blue. Because when I see that color, all I can see is that fucking redheaded monster.

All I can hear is my baby screaming from behind the bedroom door."

Pause.

"I've never told anybody about that — not any of it, but especially the sky part. The cerulean blue."

We got to his street before mine, and Gus did hug me. And as it turned out, he was true to his word. We never did talk about it again.

12

It was only about 25 percent done the next time I crossed over, but the death strip seemed to fascinate the border guards on the beach. The East German guards and the Polish guards were just walking around in the middle of it, chatting. I could hear them from the part of the woods that still existed, the part where I secreted myself. I was able to peek out at one point and get a glimpse of them sitting on tree stumps that hadn't yet been removed, sitting and laughing, undoubtedly straining to make their dirty jokes understood in the others' language.

I could tell that this was going to be my last trip through the woods. In another month, they'd be done clearing the space. It was about 40 yards wide — 20 yards on each side of the border. A new fence would undoubtedly follow the clearing of the trees, a fence that would stretch the 400 feet from the promenade to the sea. The idea of running 20 yards in the open, getting over the fence, and then running another 20 yards without being seen by either the East German or Polish guards seemed a fantasy. And if they installed even a cursory bit of lighting, well, forget it.

Nightmare in Poland

This really might have been my last trip to Swinoujscie, and I wondered if I had to tell Father Pete. It would likely gut him, but maybe not. Just as I was kind of hoping for a way out, maybe he was, too. Maybe that's all he needed, an outside excuse where he could convince himself that he wasn't the one doing the quitting, that I was quitting on him instead.

The biddies were backed up at the confessional like cars caught in a traffic jam, but Pete moved them along smartly. He lingered more than about three minutes with only one of them, a younger biddy who had retained a bit of her figure. For Pete's entertainment, I hoped she was confessing to using that figure in some illicit fashion.

Finally, as the last of them finished saying their penance up at the altar rail, I knelt down and he opened the screen.

"That one was kind of a hot mama, you know, for an old lady," I said.

"I don't know what you're talking about," Pete said.

"I can hear it in your voice — you're fucking lying. Tell me what she did. Give a pal a break."

"The seal of the confessional, pal. You know I can't—"

"Above the waist or below. You can give me that much."

"Both," he said, and we both burst out laughing. It was loud enough that Pete looked around to see if anyone was near enough to hear, but the church was empty. Then, he said, "God, I'm going to hell."

"You seem like you're in a better mood," I said.

"I'm not. Trust me, I'm not."

With that, he rattled off his latest series of observations. Most were beyond useless, but there was a pony amid the shit: two new gun emplacements at the entrance to the harbor.

"They're really big — much bigger than the others near the shipyard," he said. "I mean, I couldn't get that close — but from what I could see, they're twice the size of the other ones. Just big, like, cannons or something. But, you know, more sophisticated than cannons. But just, fucking big. It took them a week to bring all the pieces in and assemble them — tons of men, big-ass cranes, for a whole week. Always at night. And with me sitting on just the right park bench, reading my breviary under the streetlight."

"Cops never question you?"

"Nah. They're all Catholic, and they all know priests have to read from the breviary every day. A lot of priests carry it around, grab a few pages here and there between sick visits and stuff. Nobody looks twice."

We talked a little more about the exact location of the guns. That was the kind of stuff, I knew, that the Gehlen people liked because that's the kind of stuff that the Americans liked, and the Americans were still paying most of the Gehlen Org bills. The only thing the Americans like better were organization charts — government agencies, Communist party hierarchies, stuff like that. But Father Pete was not in that business.

He sensed my interest in the information he did provide, though, and that seemed to pep him up — well, for a few minutes, anyway. But then it was like somebody just flipped a switch and he was back to being nervous, morose, depressed, panicked — take your pick.

And then, Pete said, "I need to tell you something."

I waited. He said nothing.

"Well?"

"Nah, forget it."

"Come on, now."

"No, forget it."

"This is absurd," I said. "Look, we're partners here. Not friends, not brothers — partners. I have an end to hold up and you have an end to hold up. We're both doing fine that way, but

you're paralyzed by something here, something in your head —
and if it gets any worse, it could get both of us killed."

"A little melodramatic, no?" he said.

"It's not fucking melodramatic. You're new at this but I'm not. You're doing good work, important work, but it can all turn to shit in a second if you're not careful — if you're depressed, distracted, whatever. And I'm telling you, distracted people in our business die. They die all the time, and there's nothing in that breviary of yours that can protect you. And if they catch you, they're going to catch me, because everybody talks in the end."

"I wouldn't," he said. He was looking down.

"You would. I would. Everybody would. When they're lopping off your fingers, one at a time, with a kitchen knife, hell. Everybody blabs. So, no, I'm not being melodramatic. If this is anything beyond general nervousness or loneliness, anything that can't be cured by a shot of vodka or a perfumed whore, I need to know."

"Christ, you're crass," Pete said.

"I'll take that as a compliment, but you're avoiding the question."

"I can be good at that," he said. And then we just started at each other through the screen for about 10 seconds.

"Not here," Pete said. He looked at his watch. "The first thing you need to do is go up to the altar rail and say your Hail Marys."

"My what?"

"Your penance for being a degenerate asshole. Five Hail Marys. It's a bargain. See if you can remember the words. Anyway, while you're praying, I'm going to lock up the church for a few minutes."

"What if somebody comes? Isn't it always open during the

day? Won't it seem strange? You don't want to create strange... anything. That might be the first rule of this life of ours."

"It'll be fine," he said. "The next Mass isn't until 8. Nobody will come before 7:45. That'll give us plenty of time. And even if somebody did come, whatever. Nobody will think twice about it. After it's locked up, you can follow me into the sacristy — that little door at the side of the altar. We'll do it in there."

PART II

13

The sacristy was the room where the priests changed into the robes they wore when saying Mass. They were all hanging in a cupboard that took up an entire wall: green, red, black, white, maybe some others. Different sizes, different colors. On the floor against the opposite wall was a safe, and Father Pete was locking up the two gold goblets he had used during the service.

"Real gold?" I said.

"It's required."

"Hence the safe."

"A genius, you are," he said.

There were two chairs, and Pete pointed me to one of them. He paced around as he began speaking. It was as if he was trying to conjure some physical momentum and hoping it would lead to some verbal momentum.

But after about 15 seconds of "well" and "you see" and "what I mean," I said, "Will you just spit it out?"

He stared me down.

"Fine — I might be in danger," Pete said.

"Physical danger?"

"Not sure."

"Then what kind of danger?"

"Just let me tell you the story. There's this priest..."

With that, Father Pete began to tell me about another priest in the rectory. He said there were four all together — him, the plant-pissing Monsignor, another priest named Adamczyk who arrived at Stella Maris a year before Pete did, and this new guy. Father Filip Dabrowski.

"He's from Krakow, and his assignment is temporary," Pete said.

"Is that odd?"

"Not in and of itself," he said. "I mean, priests are known to go on temporary assignments all the time. Maybe to replace a priest who's recovering from an illness, or on some kind of compassionate leave, or maybe to fill in for a go-getter who's spending a semester at university working on an advanced degree. But we've got none of those things."

"Okay, but—"

"And here's the other thing," Pete said. "The temporary guys are usually either kids right out of the seminary or semi-retired old guys. Dabrowski is neither. He's, like, my age."

"Still, that doesn't—" I said, and Pete stopped me again. He was rolling now.

"A, we don't need him. B, he doesn't fit the profile. And C — I know it's just a feeling — but the guy, he's a busybody. But it's more than that, more than a busybody. He snoops — like, actively snoops. The mail delivery every day has nothing to do with him — it's the parish mail, not personal mail — but I caught him leafing through the stack the other day."

"That hardly seems like—"

"Like I said, it's just a feeling. I don't have evidence that would stand up in a court of law or anything. But it's just... like, he just disappears some nights. Says he likes to take the night air. But for three hours?"

"Maybe he has a girl."

Pete shook his head.

"A fella?"

"Shut up and listen," he said. "I followed him one night. He went into town. He went into a bar on the same street as the security barracks. They're three doors apart."

"Again, might be a simple explanation," he said. "You know, he likes to take a drink."

"You can do that here in the rectory — you're supposed to do that here in the rectory. Those are the rules. They teach you in the seminary, in so many words, that if you have impure thoughts, best to take care of them in your own room. And if you want to drink to forget your impure thoughts, same thing. And if you're going out to dinner, you do it in threes, not twos."

"They write that down in a manual or something?"

"Like I said, in so many words."

"But what you've told me," I said. "I mean, forget about holding up in a court of law. It wouldn't hold up in a drunken conversation. All you've given me is a feeling."

"I'm telling you—"

"Look," I said. "I believe in feelings, too. I believe, after you've done our thing for a little while, that you do develop a little bit of a sixth sense in situations, and that you should pay attention to it. So I'm listening. But, shit, you've given me nothing. I need more."

Pete was pacing back and forth in the sacristy when he started but was now kind of working in a circle. He was almost making me dizzy. But he never stopped walking, not for a second.

"He's just so nosy," Pete said. "Like, he's always asking me where I'm from, when I was born, where I went to school, on and on."

"Like you said, he's a busybody. I mean, other than the obvious, you don't have anything to hide, do you?"

Pete didn't answer. He also, finally, stopped pacing and dropped into the chair opposite me.

"A girl?"

No answer.

"A fella?"

No answer.

"What, then?"

No answer. Head down. Deep breath. Rub the temples. Deep breath. Rub the eyes.

Head up, finally.

"What are you hiding?"

"A dead man," Pete said.

"Quite dead?"

"Permanently dead."

"And how did he get permanently dead?" I said.

At that, Father Pete stood up, and walked across the sacristy, and opened a cabinet door, and reached inside, and poured us each a measure of something amber. It was nice. Priests drink the good stuff, even at 7 a.m.

14

I gave us each the respite of a first sip of the smooth, strong liquor, and then a second. And then, I said, "All right, out with it."

Pete was sitting now. No pacing.

"You know how I told you that nobody's ever given me a second look?" he said. "That I sit on the bench and read my breviary and nobody pays me any mind? Well, there was this one time. Like, six months ago."

"Pretty soon after you started, then."

"Yeah, yeah," Pete said. "I took the normal precautions, the ones we talked about. I walked a different route every time. I didn't always head toward the shipyard. Sometimes I just wandered aimlessly, kind of directed by nothing. Like, I had entire nights when I didn't go within a half-mile of the shipyard. I really just walked and read those nights. Maybe I saw a couple of the UB men in uniform, and I just followed them from like a block behind. That's how I found out where the barracks was."

"The one on the same street as the bar your priest drinks in," I said.

"Exactly. So, like that. And I really wasn't doing anything but wandering around this one night. Like I said, one of those nothing nights — nowhere near the shipyard. Just walking and thinking and reading. I had the breviary and I really did want to finish a couple of pages, and I sat on a bench and dug into it. Like I said, I wasn't near anything worth knowing about — not the shipyard, not the lighthouse, really not anything. Just a little park — really, not that far from here. Between here and the beach. You've made that walk. You've probably passed it and never thought twice about it. There's nothing there — just houses, a couple of guest houses, a restaurant or two. Just normal shit."

"And you were just sitting there, reading…"

"And this plainclothes guy kind of rousts me, says he's Lieutenant Such-and-Such from the UB, and that he's bringing me in for questioning. That his car is on the next street, and that he wants me to walk there with him, and that he hopes I don't give him any trouble. Then he pats his pocket, like he has a gun."

"And I said to him, as calmly as I could, 'Can I ask you why, Lieutenant?' And he said, 'Sure, Father. I'll tell you when we get there.'"

With that, Father Pete said, he and the UB agent began walking. He said they were pretty much side by side, with the priest maybe half a pace ahead of Lieutenant Such-and-Such.

He said, "I was shitting myself, but I'm pretty sure if anybody saw us, they wouldn't get that sense. We were both in our uniforms, as it were, and somebody passing the other way might see that as odd. But other than that, nothing. Just two people walking together and taking the night air."

Pete said, based on the route that the UB guy was taking, that he was pretty sure he knew where they were going. He had identified the UB barracks but not the offices, or headquarters, or whatever you called it. But he had an idea what block it was on, and that's where they seemed to be heading.

"So, it's night — and not that bright of a night," Father Pete said. "Quarter-moon, something like that. And if we were heading where I thought we were heading, there would be a good three or four minutes where we walking along the canal. You've done that, right?"

"Tell me," I said.

"Well, it's a canal."

"Asshole."

"It's a canal, but the bank isn't neat and straight. There are a lot of, I don't know, indentations and overgrown spots — and no street lights. It's pretty well known that these are the spots where the upstanding young men of Swinoujscie often discover the delights that are released with the flick of a bra strap."

"Why, Father. I'm blushing."

"Hearing confessions does have its entertaining moments," he said. "Anyway, those three or four minutes along the canal, I figured that was my shot. So I casually stuck the breviary under my armpit and began to walk with my hands jammed into my coat pockets. The knife was in my right-hand pocket."

"Your what?" I said.

"My knife. A kitchen knife. Actually, a steak knife. There were 12 of them in the drawer. Nobody would miss one."

"Jesus. And?"

"And it was easier than I ever imagined it would be," Pete said. "He was wearing a suit jacket, and it was unbuttoned, and I knew the shirt was my target. If I hit the jacket, my odds would decrease. And I knew that the belly was probably the best way to go — I read somewhere you bleed more there. Yes?"

"Maybe," I said.

"Anyway, I just turned as if to ask him something and stuck him as hard as I could, right above the belt. He was stunned, and he tried to fight me but more just kind of fell on me. I pulled out the knife and got him again on the side of his neck, and that was it. We were about 20 feet from one of those hidden copses along the water, and I rolled him out of sight. And then I threw the knife as far as I could into the canal."

"Christ, you must have been covered in blood," I said.

"Black cassock, dark night," he said. "I mean, I nearly did shit myself when I walked home — like, literally shit myself. But I surprised myself with how I kept it together. Walk fast, but not too fast. Five minutes in — like, maybe three blocks from here — I realized."

"What?"

"The breviary," he said. "So I had to walk back and look for it in the grass in the dark. It took a minute, but I found it. And then I walked back, and got a shower, and threw away the cassock, and..."

We were finishing our second portions of the good stuff. He held up the bottle — a question.

"What the hell," I said.

"Exactly," he said, and he poured us both a bit more. I had a half-dozen questions, but I sat on them and just looked at the priest as I drank. I always knew they were just men, after all, and maybe all men have the murder-a-secret-police-lieutenant gene in their makeup. Still, I could only shake my head — a little in admiration but mostly in wonder.

"When did they find him?" I said.

"No idea."

"No newspaper story?"

"Not that I saw."

"And you never went back to check?"

"Hell, no," he said. "Should I have?"

"Hell, no," I said.

They found him — there was no way they wouldn't have, especially if the canal was as popular with teenagers as Pete believed. It might have taken a few days, but somebody found him — either a couple of horny 16-year-olds or, more likely, an old man walking his dog. There wasn't any question there.

"And nobody's asked you about it?" I said.

"Nobody?"

"UB, regular cops, the postman?"

"Nobody," Pete said.

"What that suggests..."

"Is that the lieutenant was freelancing..."

"Exactly," I said. "It must not have been a planned thing that night. You're not in the books at headquarters anywhere. He just saw you and figured he might bust your balls."

"Because he could."

"It's one of the privileges of the job."

The priest nodded. The UB was in the business of collecting information and creating an atmosphere of terror. They were to be feared, and everybody needed to know it if the system was going to hold together.

Which got me to the main question.

"So, I get that it's likely the most traumatic event of your life," I said. "But you got away with it by all accounts. If they haven't come for you all these months later, they're not coming for you now. So, well, what is it?"

Pete looked down into his empty glass.

"So, who knows?" I said.

"Well," he said.

"I'll ask my same two questions. A girl? A fella?"

Pete shook his head.

"Come on."

"The pastor," he said.

"The drunken plant pisser? Why in the world..."

"He's my confessor," Pete said.

"Christ. What are you doing? In this business..."

"In this business, I like to think I'm doing the Lord's work, protecting the church against these... these... But nobody told me I had to give up my faith. And, like I said, he's my confessor. He can't talk about it, obviously."

"But..."

"He's just drunk so much," Pete said. "And that nosy goddamned Dabrowski. Maybe I'm being paranoid. I don't know."

I didn't know what to tell him. When I went for the joke — maybe he's so drunk that he thinks he dreamed it — it fell flat.

"You know how I told you I threw away my cassock from that night and my shoes and my socks and my skivvies?" Father Pete said. He walked over to where his coat was hanging and reached into the pocket. The breviary. He opened the back cover and, on the inside, there was a dark brown stain — more of a smear. Dried blood.

"I couldn't throw this away. I mean, I just couldn't. And I see this every time I read it, and my heart kind of skips," he said.

15

Father Pete checked his watch.
"I should go unlock the door," he said.
"How long till the next Mass?"
"Twenty minutes. Twenty-one."
"Are you...?"
"No, Adamczyk. Come on, walk me out."

We left the sacristy and walked down the middle aisle of the small church. When we got to the end, Pete bent over and straightened out the red carpet runner that covered the floor.

"More trouble than it's worth," he mumbled. "Old ladies trip on the rug more than they slip when the bare floor is wet."

He unlocked the door, opened it, and looked outside. Nobody waiting. The two of us walked out to the sidewalk. Pete looked back at the church — narrow, red brick, with "Ave Maris Stella" in gold letters high above the door and the round stained-glass window.

"Ave Maris Stella," Pete said. "Hail, Star of the Sea. It's a prayer for travelers. German, Polish — it's been a church for the fishermen, and the guys in the shipyard, and the other people who made their living from the Baltic, from the sea."

He stopped, and his voice caught.

"Alex, what the hell am I going to do?"

"I would tell you to keep drinking, but not that stuff — three little glasses and I'm already on my ass. It isn't even 8 a.m.," I said.

He smiled, weakly.

"The way I see it, you're not in any danger. You did what you did — and for the record, with the same steak knife in my pocket, I probably would have done the same thing. Whether I would have pulled it off is another matter entirely. But the point is, you did pull it off. There's no reason to think otherwise."

"Except..."

"Except for Nosy Dabrowski and the drunken Monsignor," I said. "I got it. I heard you. But you really don't have anything concrete, just your unsettled feelings. And, we both have to be honest — it might just be your conscience causing the anxiety."

"It's really not."

"How can you be sure?"

"I've had a guilty conscience before."

"Well, now I'm interested."

"Fuck you," he said, but with a smile. "You don't need any details — other than that it was during the war, and there were bombs literally falling all around us, and in those kinds of circumstances..."

I waved my hand.

"Is that all? I said.

"A big deal for me. But I know how I felt afterward — and this ain't that."

"Killing a guy is different than..."

"I like to think of it as self-defense."

"As you should. Because that's what it was."

"And that's the point," he said. "It was a terrible thing but that's exactly what it was — self-defense during wartime. I mean, I consider this wartime or I wouldn't be involved. So, like, my conscience is clear."

"Then why did you confess it to the Monsignor?"

"I don't know — force of habit, I guess. Or just, well, maybe I just needed to tell somebody."

"He must have been shocked."

"He was actually good," Father Pete said. "It was early, before he was drinking. And the old man, I mean, he's seen some shit. He fought in the first war, before the seminary."

"I did, too," I said.

"Yeah, but you must have been a kid with a gun and no hair on your balls. He was an officer. Like I said, he saw some shit. And when I told him, he just got quiet for a second and then he said, 'It never ends, does it?' And then, he said, 'I cannot absolve you for a sin that you didn't commit. But I'm going to do it anyway, just in case.' And then he laughed, and I laughed, and we both said at the same time, 'Just in case.' And then we got drunk together in the rectory."

"He sounds like a good man," I said. "You really think he'd violate his oath and tell Dabrowski?"

"He's forgetting his underwear and pissing in potted plants, Alex. I mean, I just don't know — but I also can't stop worrying about it."

A parishioner approached as we stood on the sidewalk. He looked at his watch and then at Pete.

"It's Father Adamczyk today, and he's never late," Pete said. The old man nodded and said, "Then I better get my spot."

We were alone again, and Pete said, "Maybe you could just keep an eye on Dabrowski for me. I mean, see what he's up to. Maybe get a better idea of what he does at night. I mean, I don't know."

My immediate reflex was to turn him down flat, but I forced myself to think about it for a few seconds. The delay was more for show than anything, though. The answer to me was obvious immediately.

"I can't do it," I said.

"Why not?"

"It's just not practical. I mean, where would I live? It's not like I can check into a hotel. The secret police..."

"The UB..."

"Yeah, the UB. If I checked into hotel, the UB would be on my ass before breakfast the next day."

"I could find you a place," he said.

"And what would be the purpose if I did stay? I mean, even if I saw Dabrowski make contact with a UB officer, how would I know? Do you know where their headquarters is? Did you ever figure that out?"

Pete shook his head. No.

"And here's the other thing," I said. "I have another existence on the other side of the border — you know that, right?"

He nodded. Then I lied and said, "You're not my only professional responsibility."

I offered three more practical reasons but they were camouflage. The truth was, I could have done it if Pete had been able to find me a place to live. But I didn't want to do it because, well, I didn't want to do it — partly because I really did think he was imagining things but mostly because I didn't want to get all the way back in.

And as we stood there on the sidewalk, and I told him to try to relax, what I really was doing was thinking about walking with Karin on the pier in Ahlbeck and picturing Lotte running toward us when she saw me holding the ice cream. I just couldn't get back in. Not all the way back.

I tried to keep that picture in my head as I walked away from Stella Maris. I had to kill the rest of the day before I slipped back over the border. Given my head start on inebriation, I decided to take a walk in the sunshine and get some breakfast and try to sober up, at least a little. After that, though, the magnetic pull of the line of crappy bars near the shipyard was too much for me to overcome. I didn't really fight very hard, truth be told — because I knew that the picture and the pier and the ice cream were long gone from my consciousness, replaced by, well, by something that would require a bit of an anesthetic.

16

I had fought against the mission to Krakow from the moment that Fritz brought it up — from then until I was in the car from Vienna to the airfield.

"Who gives a fuck about a fucking chemical plant?" is what I asked more or less a dozen times as Fritz laid out the plan.

"Will you listen to yourself?" Fritz said.

"I'm serious. What do they make out of chemicals?"

"Fertilizer, mostly — for them and also for Mother Russia. And having an idea about the state of the Soviet farming capabilities, it matters."

"To who?"

"Don't be obtuse."

"Fuck obtuse. Who?"

"The Americans. They pay the bills and they want to know. And why you made me say it out loud when you knew all along..."

"Always important to establish who has your balls in their pocket," I said. "In fact, I think you're the first one I ever heard say that."

"Smart ass."

"At your service."

We had both been drinking pretty hard. We were at the American

Bar in Vienna, one of my old favorites, a hole-in-the-wall near the cathedral. It reminded me of the old days, the days when I was young, the days before Hitler, when my major concern at the American Bar was getting drunk quickly with my friends before the pursuit of female companionship for the evening commenced. Twenty-five years since then. A quarter-century. Jesus.

Fritz was laying out the assignment. Hyman Pietroski, Auschwitz survivor, was a draftsman. He had access to the plans for a new chemical plant that the Poles were planning to build in Jerzmanowice — plans that included production capabilities for fabricating different chemicals, particularly fertilizers.

"Which can be converted, with a little tweak, into bombs, by the way," Fritz said.

"Atomic bombs?"

"No, just normal bombs."

"Which aren't shit anymore."

"Unless you're sitting on one when it blows," he said. "But that's neither here nor there. It's the fertilizer. It's the arithmetic of agriculture that some eggheads will do — x-tons of fertilizer will lead to x-thousands of bushels of wheat from Ukraine. Like that."

"So, just get this Hyman Whatshisname to tell one of your Polish operatives how many tons, and he can radio it out, and I can have another drink here."

"It's not that simple."

"The fuck it's not."

"They want the plans. They heard the word 'blueprints' and I thought they were going to shoot in their trousers."

"They?"

"Fuck you."

"Okay, the almighty 'They' want the plans. Then Hyman Whatshisname delivers them to your Polish op and I sit here in the American Bar and relive the exploits of my youth."

"Ancient history."

"Tell me about it. But, seriously. Why me?"

Fritz waved and got us two more Manhattans. We were already three deep and in danger of having to walk home on our knees. But, well.

"We have two men in Krakow," Fritz said. "And I use the term loosely. One of them likely doesn't have any hair on his balls yet. Says he's nineteen, but we don't believe him. And the other is, well, let's just say that he's not known as a people person."

"What the hell does that mean?"

"It's hard to explain. I've actually met him, and he's fine for following orders. He's careful. He'll have no trouble emptying the dead drop and moving the plans along the line. But he's, like, shy. Can't look you in the eye. Can't carry on a conversation. And your guy, Hyman Pietroski, he's going to need some hand-holding. He's nervous, a little bit scared. More than a little."

We both stopped and took a long drink, and I debated in my head. On the one hand, this is what I did for a living — and Gehlen paid well, not that I needed the money. But lacking a real job, and a family, and a life — a real life — the undercover existence was all I had. It was all I understood. I had recently read a story about somebody getting out of prison after decades and not being able to cope outside, and the person who wrote the story seemed kind of astounded — but I got it. I got it immediately. At that point in my life, Gehlen was all I had.

So, I kept running the whole thing through my alcohol-preserved brain, and then it hit me.

"Wait a minute — who recruited him?"

Fritz looked down and smiled.

"Well... I guess I was hoping you wouldn't notice that part."

"Until I'd agreed."

"Right."

"So, who recruited him?"

"The 19-year-old."

"With no hair on his balls."

"Yeah."

"And where is he now? And why can't he just carry on? I mean, if he could recruit the guy..."

"Because he's dead," Fritz said.

"What?"

"Dead? You've heard of the concept, yes? Dead."

"How?"

"Drunk, hit by a car."

"Jesus."

"Not so suspicious," Fritz said. "Out with his mates, celebrating something or other, stumbled off of the wrong curb at the wrong moment. We think it was nothing nefarious. Just bad fucking luck."

"You think?"

"Yeah, we think."

"I need more than that."

"Best I can do," Fritz said. "You know that. We never deal in certainties. We're always playing the percentages. And, well, anyway, the kid was actually pretty good. I was lying about that part. He made the contact — Hyman was the neighbor of a school chum — and set up a communications dead drop. The shy guy has been answering Hyman's notes as if he's the dead kid, but that can only go on for so long."

"And when Hyman Whatshisname finds out his contact is suddenly, unexpectedly, very much dead — come on, Fritz. He'll shit himself and then he'll run — unless he runs first and then shits himself. This is over."

"It's why we need you," he said.

"It's not salvageable if Hyman is as nervous as you say."

"It's why we need you," Fritz said, again.

He had me and he knew it. From about the second drink on, the whole conversation was performance art — Fritz playing the kindly professor, me being the recalcitrant asshole student. That we both knew I was going to agree with the wisdom of Professor Fritz in the end was all in the script. And so, after a while, the tone changed and I capitulated without ever actually saying, 'OK, I agree.' We just starting talking about the operational details — how long he thought I would be in Krakow, and the location of the dead drop, and where I would live. Fritz said the whole thing would take two months, tops — and that we would go over the details in the morning when we were sober.

"Maybe afternoon," I said.

"Early afternoon. The car for Kautzen leaves at two. I'll ride with you."

"Kautzen?"

"The airfield."

"Tomorrow?"

"Has to be," Fritz said, and then he looked down at the glass he was holding with both hands. It was empty. He waved for two more Manhattans, and we drank for several minutes in silence.

And then, I said, "Is it more dangerous than you're letting on?"

And then, Fritz said, "It's always more dangerous than I let on. But you already knew that."

17

The death strip was, indeed, finished by the next month, including the hanging of some half-assed spotlights. I was going to need another way across the border into Poland. When I went for a walk one morning on the beach, I was able to peer into the cleared area and see that they were already past the promenade and continuing to cut down trees on the other side. The East German guard didn't mind as I got to the fence and leaned over to look. The death strip had apparently become a bit of a tourist attraction.

I couldn't see how much farther they had cleared the forest because of what must have been a bend in the border. I could guess, but it would only be that, a guess. And, well, improving my intelligence didn't seem possible in the three days I had until my next visit to Swinoujscie.

Which left me with the Baltic. And with Gerd Fromm, who was doing what he was always doing when I walked by him on the beach in Ahlbeck. He was fussing with something on the fishing boat, always fussing — nets, engine, painting. Fussing. It was the nets this day — untangling here, re-tying there.

He produced a bottle after a while, and we sat on some rocks and passed it back and forth. He asked about Karin and Lotte and wondered when I would bring them around again. I promised him it would be soon. We talked about the weather, which had been unusually benign. We grew quiet, and I watched the little waves lap up to the shoreline.

"Are you going to ask me?" Gerd said.

"Ask you what?"

"Whatever the hell you came to ask me," he said.

"Well," I said. And after a few seconds: "Well, if somebody wanted to get into Poland, could you help get them there? You know, quietly?"

He leaned back, and then he pushed cap back a little bit to expose more of his forehead.

"Where in Poland?" Gerd said.

"Swinoujscie."

"Like, right over there," he said, and then he pointed along the shore.

"Right over there," I said.

I had wondered ahead of time what I would say if Gerd asked me why. In the end, I decided that I wasn't going to lie — I was just going to refuse to answer. But he never asked. In the course of the next few minutes, there were several awkward silences and several times when he took off the cap and scratched the top of his head. But Gerd never asked.

After one particularly long pull on the bottle, he said, "It's really pretty easy. In theory, we're supposed to go straight out for three miles. That far out, nobody cares what we do. Closer than that, in theory, we're crossing imaginary border lines."

"In theory?" I said.

"Yeah. The truth is, more than about a mile with your lights off is fine. Their patrols are much closer to the shoreline than that, and they really couldn't be all that bothered. So, maybe a mile and a half, and I drop you and the dinghy over the side, and that's that."

"The dinghy?"

"Rubber. Small. Fine in calm waters, useless in a storm — but the weather report says it's going to be like this for, like, five more days. Benign. Calm."

"So, I just beach it?"

"No," Gerd said. "I'd say, I don't know, a hundred yards out or so, you puncture the dinghy and do your best to sink it when the air is all out. It's no big deal either way, I don't think, but you want to sink it. And then you swim in the rest of the way. You can swim, right?"

I nodded.

"But I'll be soaked," I said. "I can't be soaked. I won't dry off in time for..."

I stopped.

Gerd looked down and scratched his head again.

"You won't be soaked, you'll be naked," he said.

"The hell?"

"What, are you shy?"

"Seriously."

"I'll give you a bag," he said. "It'll be made of oilcloth. You put your clothes in there — there's a zippered compartment inside — and then you tie the bag closed, then tie the whole thing kind of up here so it's on your back."

He pointed to his upper chest.

"It's not perfect, but the stuff will stay dry enough as long as you aren't in the water for too long. And you won't be. Like I said, maybe a hundred yards."

Three nights later, I was standing on the deck of his fishing boat, stripping down and filling the oilcloth bag. Gerd could see I was skeptical and said, "Don't worry. It'll work."

Then, he handed me a small knife.

"For puncturing the dinghy. One hole on each side, just to speed it up."

Then, he handed me a small pistol.

"A lady gun, Gerd?"

"You fucking want it or not?"

I took it, opened the zippered compartment, and shoved the gun into one of my boots.

"It's really not necessary," I said.

"Look," Gerd said. "I haven't asked you what this is about and I'm not going to ask you. Because, well, I'm a decent judge of character, and, well..."

"I'm not an asshole?"

"You're a righteous asshole."

"I'm honored."

"You should be," Gerd said. "That might be the highest compliment I'm capable of giving. So listen to me, righteous asshole. I see how Karin looks at you. And I especially see how Lotte looks at you. They are damaged people, Alex. So I'm not asking what this is about and I don't want to know. I really don't. But I'm doing what I can to get you there. How you get back, that's on you. But get back. Get back for those two. Back in one piece."

He stopped.

"You are coming back, right?" he said.

"I am."

"For them," he said.

About five minutes later, we were far enough out into the Baltic. I was freezing, hugging myself, even thought it was a fairly mild night. Gerd had navigated without his lights, not that it was very difficult. All he had to do was go a mile out and a mile to the right. The lights of Swinoujscie and especially the shipyard were visible, even that late.

"How long?" he said.

"Just a day. You sure I can't just stash the dinghy somewhere?"

"You tell me. Do you know the beach there? Is it patrolled? How close are the dunes? I haven't been there in like 15 years, but my memory of when it was Swinemünde was that there were overgrown dunes right next to the border but not so much in the town. Like, not at all. And if you couldn't hide it in the dunes, I don't know where."

I nodded and said nothing. I didn't want to tell him that I had been making the monthly trip to Swinoujscie for a while, and that his memory was good. There really was nowhere to hide the dinghy except right next to the border — and I couldn't be that close.

He lowered the dinghy into the water and I got ready to climb down a rope ladder that, honestly, didn't look like it would hold my weight.

"I'd hug you but I'm naked," I said.

"Asshole."

"Righteous asshole."

"Just regular asshole," Gerd said.

18

The whole thing went off pretty much uneventfully, except that I almost strangled myself when I attempted to tie the oilcloth bag around my upper torso and ended up, after a few swimming strokes, feeling the rope creep up around my neck. But here's the thing about the Baltic: it takes forever to get really deep. If you watch families playing in the water on a Sunday, the dads and the teenage boys can easily go out 150 feet, maybe more, and still be only up to their necks. It might have been 15 feet deep where I punctured the dinghy, and closer to 10 feet when the rope started scaring me. Ten feet. That's oddly reassuring, even as you struggle with the thought of strangling yourself in the sea.

I never panicked — well, not full-on panic — mostly because I never considered the stories about drunks who fell down on their faces and drowned in a puddle of water along the curb. Ten feet. I could handle 10 feet. The reality was that I ended up walking about half of the distance and holding the oilcloth bag over my head. I didn't think about the drunks and the puddles until I was back on the beach, air-drying and shivering for a few minutes before I slipped into my clothes.

I stopped off at one of the shipyard bars for a beer or two. This wasn't going to be the easiest conversation. I was cutting off Father Pete, after all. There was no way I was going to keep this up, not with the death strip. There weren't enough dinghies in the world to get me to do that — and God knows how I was going to get back to East Germany as it was. No, this was it — and it didn't matter how spooked he was or who he thought he might be seeing in the shadows.

The truth was, he might be relieved. I mean, if he didn't have a contact anymore to take his information, there was no need to gather the information anymore. I was setting him adrift, yes, but it gave him the perfect out. For all I knew, he might kiss me.

I got to Stella Maris a little late; okay, it was three beers. The Mass was letting out of the narrow brick church — three old ladies, two old men, one shipyard worker in overalls and carrying his lunch. I went inside and saw a big guy in the confessional, and there was nobody else waiting. For some reason, I looked at the guy before I looked at Father Pete. Except, it wasn't Father Pete.

I thought for a second — was this the wrong day? But only for a second, because I knew it wasn't. We had never missed connections before, and that raised all kinds of alarm bells. He had been worried, and there was the nosy substitute priest in the rectory, and there was the UB guy that Pete had killed, and oh fuck...

I could feel my heart racing as I tried to think. Then I was distracted by the sight of the guy getting up from the kneeler, leaving the confessional, and heading to the altar rail to say his Hail Marys. Big, tall guy in a uniform. Big, tall guy in a uniform with red hair.

In a millisecond, my mind jumped to Gus Braun, and his wife, and his daughter, and the big, redheaded security soldier who...

And what was his name? I couldn't remember.

My heart was still pounding, and now my mind was in several places at once, and then I heard the priest say, "Oh, I didn't see you. Are you prepared?"

"Prepared for what?"

"Have you examined your conscience?"

"No, Father," I said. I was in a full panic. Which priest was this — the nosy guy or the other guy? I didn't think he was the drunken monsignor because he seemed to young. And, you know, not drunk.

"No offense, Father, but my confessor is Father..."

I stopped. I couldn't remember his last name.

"Father Pete," I said. "Like I said, no offense. But do you know where he is?"

The priest went quiet and looked down at his shoes.

"Father, he is a friend as well as my confessor."

"He's gone," the priest said. "Don't know where. Just gone. Two weeks now. He has an uncle in Krakow, but no. We called. Just gone. And now with Father Dabrowski transferred back to Krakow, it's hectic."

Gone?

What?

If gone meant arrested, then I was in danger. I realized that immediately. I needed to get back to East Germany — that night. It was that much of an emergency. I needed to find a way back over the border, and that would be that. If it was a dark enough night, maybe I could just walk in the water of the Baltic when it was up to my neck. A dark night, maybe. Christ, what was the moon last night? I didn't even remember.

So, get out — although the truth was, I wasn't positive that East Germany would be safe, either. Because even if the East Germans and the Poles were wary allies, that didn't mean the UB didn't have at least a bit of a working relationship with the

Stasi. And the problem was that, over the months, Father Pete and I had become too chummy. He didn't know all of the details — didn't know I lived in Ahlbeck or that I worked at The Denkler — but he knew I had been in Heringsdorf. I had mentioned Heringsdorf. The dangers of chumminess.

"I'm sorry," the priest said. He left me to sit alone in the back pew. If Pete had been gone for two week, well, two weeks equaled dead. If the UB boys were just scaring him, or sweating him, it would be over either way in a couple of days. Two weeks, though. Dead.

That's when the wave of what-ifs arrived, and they came closer to drowning me than the Baltic. What if I had agreed to Father Pete's request to come live in Swinoujscie and watch his back for a while? What if I had cut him loose earlier, knowing the dangers tended to grow exponentially when amateurs stayed in the field too long? What if I had taught him better? What if I had asked Fritz to try to gather a little intel on the nosy priest, Dabrowski? And, by the by, what did it mean that Dabrowski had just been transferred back to Krakow?

I looked down and realized I was kneeling, even if I didn't remember getting off my ass. I noticed that my heart rate had calmed even as the ache in my chest grew. And then I saw the big redhead stand up at the altar rail and turn to walk down the aisle. He looked at his wristwatch and then he began to walk quickly. A busy man, maybe late for a meeting.

I stared straight ahead, as if praying.

His eyes were fixed beyond me, on the door and whatever he was late for.

On my knees, my eyes were chest level as he hurried by.

I saw the nameplate.

Carney.

Yes, that was the name Gus mentioned.

Carney.

19

Without thinking, I counted to 20 and followed Carney. Given his size and his hair, he was easy enough to spot, even from nearly a block behind. He walked for about 10 minutes, left here, right there, and ended up walking into a smallish building that looked like it was offices — stone, squat, three stories tall. I assumed it was the UB headquarters but I couldn't be positive. There was a chance that Carney was NKVD instead. That seemed a longer shot, granted, but if a Carney could be an officer in Polish state security, it wasn't impossible that a Carney could be in the Soviet security police.

I didn't know what to do, so I went to the beach. It was a little chilly but sunny, and I took off my shirt and closed my eyes and tried not to be overwhelmed by the sound of my beating heart. I tried to focus on the waves that gently rolled into the shoreline. There was a nice, easy, regular cadence, and it did relax me for a second. I listened to the waves and then to my breathing. In, out. In, out. And then, in the same cadence, what I heard in my head was "Oh, shit, oh, shit..."

I had no idea how I was going to get home to Ahlbeck that

night and I couldn't even think of anything besides taking off my clothes, rolling them up into a ball of sorts, and walking out into the water as far as I could with the bundle resting on my head. A hundred and fifty feet, give or take, out into the Baltic. But would that be enough? Especially near the border strip, where the guards lingered on either side? And would there be patrols in the water? Just because I hadn't seen any the previous night, well, who knew? And the moon...

The alternative was going through the woods overland, but I had no clue how far south of the promenade they had extended the death strip — and I also had no idea where a safe place to enter the woods might be, or what the border security situation might be. That was true on both sides. Even if I managed to worm may way into the forest on the Polish side, I had no way of knowing what might await me on the East German side for the deworming.

Somehow, I think I actually did sleep for a while as all of this swirled in my head. Then a late breakfast. Then two beers. Then a late lunch. Then two beers. And then, for reasons that still weren't clear to me, I found a bench in the park across the street from the three-story office building that Gus Braun's redheaded nightmare had entered hours earlier. It was coming up on 4 p.m. If Carney was a desk officer, there was a decent chance that he was still in there. If he was a field officer, well, who knew?

What I was doing there, and what I might do if I saw him, really was a mystery. I was reacting more than thinking, allowing years of instincts to override what still, even all these years later, was a kind of inborn hesitancy about getting involved. My Uncle Otto had it, too. He took care of the woman he loved in his will, and he took care of her in life, too — but he never married her and he never even spent an entire night in her apartment. It was as if he always had one eye on the escape hatch, and that was the way he lived his life. And for a long time, that was the way I lived my life, too, before Czech intelligence contacted me and asked for help as a courier between them and dissident German army officers before the start of the second war. That was 1937 or 1938 — I always forgot — and I have been involved ever since, but the one-eye-on-the-escape-hatch part of my personality was never entirely squelched.

That day, though, my instincts ruled. And at 4:25, when Carney and two of his co-workers left the office, and walked down the block, and entered a bar called The Night Watchman, I waited five minutes and then followed them in.

The Night Watchman. Seeing as how virtually all of Swinoujscie — the bombed-out part and the rest — was depopulated of Germans and repopulated with Poles in the years after the war, my guess was that the bar owner was either a former UB officer or maybe a relative, because the name was just too perfect for the location. The Night Watchmen would have been even more perfect, come to think of it.

It was pretty dark inside even though the sun had another hour, probably. I was worried that the place would be 100 percent uniforms or black trench coats, but there was enough of a mix of soldiers and civilians that I didn't feel out of place.

I grabbed a bar stool and stuck with the beers that I had begun drinking, oh, 10 hours earlier. Carney was with his buddies at a table that was behind me — but I could hear them. Not the words, but the laughing roars every few minutes. I was glad I couldn't see them in a way because I would have been tempted to stare. I mean, I had seen plenty of human failing in my line of work — and plenty of evil, too. But this guy, this redhead, this Carney — I wasn't sure I had words for his level of evil.

Two beers became three, and three became four, and four became I-lost-count — and they were still at the table in the back corner.

Every few minutes, usually after one of the group guffaws, my mind wandered back. Father Pete. Fuck. Disappeared without a word could mean only one thing. Well, two — either UB or NKVD. It wasn't hard to see that one or the other caught him taking one too many clandestine walks near a military facility at night. And if they ever got a whiff that he had been the one to kill that guy along the canal, well. The truth was, Pete likely gave it all up before they killed him, and that he likely considered his death to be a blessing at that point. He was in the death-as-a-blessing business, after all.

Which also meant he likely gave me up. In the same circumstances, I probably would have given him up, too. I'd like to think I was better than that, but who was I kidding? With an electric wire clipped to my balls, it wouldn't take more than one jolt of current to turn me into a blabbering coward. We all had our things, our fears, and that was mine. And because I had just thought about it during the day, I undoubtedly would think about it at night. There were periods of my life where I thought about electric wires and testicles — specifically my testicles — every time I turned off the lights at night. I hadn't been in one of those periods, not for a while, but...

Roar, group guffaw — and then the scraping of chairs, wooden legs on linoleum. Carney and his friends were leaving.

20

The three of them said their goodbyes on the sidewalk, and then one of them turned to the left and Carney and the other one turned to the right. I saw all of that through the front window, while I shucked on my jacket. I took my time, buttoned up deliberately, and then left the bar. Left the bar and turned to the right.

Carney and the other guy were more than a block ahead of me. But there was enough of a moon that I didn't have any trouble seeing them. About three blocks from the bar, Carney clapped the other guy on the shoulder and turned right. He was headed in the direction of the canal — and, maybe three minutes later, he reached the waterline and turned left onto the street that paralleled the shoreline.

I picked up my pace and closed the distance between us. I was maybe 200 feet behind and narrowing the gap. There was enough wind blowing, and enough other ambient noise, that I didn't think he could hear my footsteps. And if I hadn't really thought it through except for one part — not the how, not the why — I knew I was going to confront the big redheaded monster, there and then.

As 200 feet became 100, and 100 became 50, and 50 became 25, I could feel the nerves — in my racing heart, in my need to fart. I closed the last bit of the gap, and took a deep breath, and then I said, "Sir, sir, you forgot this in the bar."

Carney turned.

I was holding the pistol that Gerd Fromm had tossed into the oilcloth sack. It was the one part of the plan I had thought about ahead of time, the gun.

The look on his face was not the fear I had anticipated. It was more, I don't know, bemusement — not a smile but not much short of one, and nothing alarming in the eyes. There was almost a twinkle in the eyes, although it was pretty dark. For some reason, he had the same look my Uncle Otto used to get before he told one of the old stories.

"Turn around," I said. After a quick search of his pockets, I couldn't find a weapon. He must be a desk man — either that or they keep the guns locked up in the office. Either way, well, whatever.

"Walk," I said.

He did.

After about a minute, we came to one of those irregular parts of the canal bank, a little jutted-out spot with two trees and a couple of bushes, no doubt one of the places Father Pete told me the high school kids went for their first adventure.

"In there," I said, pointing the pistol.

"With the beer bottles and the spent condoms?"

"In there."

"You think you're a tough guy, don't you?" Carney said. The arrogance of the guy was stunning. I couldn't decide if it was his basic personality of if it was the alcohol talking. I knew it was probably both, actually. Asshole plus alcohol equals a truly outrageous piece of shit. I'd seen it before.

"Tough guy? This says I'm a tough guy," I said, waving the

pistol. With that, Carney walked into the little area between the trees. I did, in fact, kick the neck of an empty beer bottle when we stopped. It made me wonder.

"Hands on top of your head, fingers laced together," I said.

"For fuck's sake..."

"Do it."

I waved the pistol, which I assumed was loaded. It felt heavy enough to be loaded. Carney did as I commanded.

"Second thought," I said. "Undo your belt and drop your trousers."

"Jesus Christ."

"Do it. Drop them around your ankles."

When he was done, standing there in his drawers, I said, "Didn't your mother tell you to wear clean underwear — you know, in case you got hit by a streetcar."

"Fuck you."

The truth was, I didn't know if they were clean or not. It was too dark for a close inspection. With that, I had him put his hands back on his head with the fingers laced. He couldn't run with his pants down, and any attempt to come at me with his hands would be telegraphed enough for me to have time to fire. I felt a bit more secure, except for when I looked at his face again. Nothing changed there. Just kind of... bemused.

I had started the conversation in German, and Carney had answered me fluently. My Polish was actually decent — I speak to Father Pete in Polish. Spoke. God. But I was worried the emotions might get the best of me and leave me searching for the right word.

"So, do you remember Gus Braun?" I said. "Wife named Connie. Daughter named Gretchen."

"Nope."

"Come on. From Swinemünde."

"Swinoujscie."

"Might still have been Swinemünde then."

"Was Swinoujscie from the day I got here."

"Whatever," I said. "Like, 1945. Gus Braun. Your partner detained him in the front room of his apartment while you raped Connie and Gretchen in the bedroom."

"Oh, for fuck's sake..."

"You raped them, and then they committed suicide a bit later. Connie and Gretchen. Braun. Nothing?"

"Other than that they were dirty fucking German whores?" Carney said. "No, nothing."

I thought about shooting him right there but I wanted to hear more. I came close to pistol-whipping him across his bemused faced but stopped myself. That was probably what he wanted. He very well could have been playing me, trying to enrage me, hoping I would get closer and make a move.

Instead, I kept my distance, maybe 10 feet.

"For a few weeks there, right at the start, it was every night," he said, with a sadistic leer. "We weren't the UB then, not officially. Just a kind of an advance guard to keep order and wait for the Red Army. Well, I mean, there were army soldiers with us — but the command, the structure, that took a while. Not that long, but a little while."

He stopped, smiled. Just enough of the moonlight came through the trees for me to see it. A smile now, soft, like for a fond memory.

"It was kind of chaos at the start but, you know, that's war, right? And at the beginning, it was every fucking night, sometimes twice a night, whoever was home. I couldn't wash the smell off my fingers for a while there. I found myself sniffing them sometimes, you know, kind of absentmindedly. You know."

"Fuck you," I said.

"What were their names? Connie and Gretchen? Filthy German whores," he said.

21

"Turn around," I said.

"What?"

"Face the water."

He complied.

"Now walk," I said.

"The fuck?"

He pointed down at the trousers gathered around his ankles.

"You'll manage," I said. He huffed but he did manage. He shuffled — trousers around ankles, hands on head, fingers laced together. It wasn't 20 feet. When he got to within about five feet of the canal, he turned.

"Happy?" he said.

"Fuck you."

"I'm glad you're behind me."

I said nothing.

"Truth is, I'm starting to get a little excited thinking about... what were their names? Connie and Gretchen? Yes, a little excited."

I knew evil. I had seen it. I had been its victim at times and I had triumphed over it at other times. Still, it always took my breath away when I was in its presence. I understood human failing, and I knew that people did things they weren't proud of, horrible things sometimes. Hell, I did own a mirror, after all. But that, to me, was sin. Sin was different than evil. This guy, this Carney, this was evil. I mean, I knew the Red Army raped its way across Germany at the end — but I liked to believe that, for most of them, it was a terrible aberration fueled by vengeance and adrenaline and, I don't know, and that there was regret in the end. This guy, though, this Carney, was different. This was a redheaded monster — even if a percentage of it was the alcohol talking.

There were a couple of big boulders along the bank of the canal, as well as a few smaller rocks — sizable but smaller.

"Sit," I said.

"Where?"

"First rock. Face the water."

Carney shuffled over and sat down.

"Hands back on your head," I said.

"Fingers laced," he said. "That's fine. You know, they'd be in my lap otherwise. Connie and Gretchen. Connie and Gretchen."

I was so upset by what he was saying that the pistol shook in my hand. The thought of Gus Braun crying when he told me the story flashed through my head, just for a second. And the bit about the blue sky. Hitler weather. Cerulean blue.

I didn't want to use the gun. I didn't even know what kind of shape it was in, really. I mean, it looked old as hell. I guessed Gerd had taken care of it — I had sniffed it when I first took it out of the oilcloth sack and could smell the gun oil — but, still. There was no visible rust but, still. When had it last been fired? In which war? It was that old. And even if it did fire properly, it was going to be loud. I didn't want loud.

I really had not planned this part out. At least, that's what I told myself. Maybe I had known all along what I was going to do. The act of confronting him was going to have consequences — that much was obvious. But there were consequences and, well, there were consequences.

Just bashing his head with the grip of the pistol and knocking him out — that was the safer play. I was thinking that — at least, that's the way I remembered it — as Carney shuffled over to the bank of the canal. One rap on the back of the head, a second for good luck, and then I'd be out of there. That's what I told myself. But then I thought about it. I had mentioned Gus Braun. The assumption that Carney made when he woke up was that Gus had been deported to Germany with the rest of the population. It was a common enough name, Braun, but if the UB and the Stasi had any kind of a reciprocal arrangement, then I had put Gus in danger. Long shot, maybe, but not no shot. That's what I told myself.

"Awfully quiet," Carney said.

I didn't answer.

"Thinking, huh? Well, I've been thinking, too. Like I told you. I don't really remember Connie and Gretchen, but maybe I do. If I'm right, the daughter, she had a mole on her thigh. It was distinctive. Cute. I mean, I was holding her down, and..."

Carney didn't finish his thought, mostly because I had reached down and picked up a rock the size of a shot-put and brained him. Once on the right temple, and his eye kind of exploded. Once on the back of the head, but it was more of glancing blow because he was falling off the rock at that point. Then once, twice, three times, more. I wasn't in control of myself after the second. I was breathing so fast, I thought I might pass out — and then I dropped the rock in the grass. At the end, his bemused face was hamburger and the rest of him was quite dead.

I looked down at my sleeves and the rest of my clothes, trying to position myself in the moonlight. I didn't see any blood.

There was some on my hands but that was all. It was a sign that I was meant to get away with it. That it was justice. That's what I told myself, too.

I rolled him over and felt for the wallet it in his hip pocket. I opened it. Piotr Carney was the name on the UB identification card. Piotr Carney. There must be a story there, about how the original Carney got to Poland and made a life. His father, his grandfather, somebody — he probably worked on the boats that came into Swinemünde and then headed downriver to Wroclaw or somewhere, and he met a girl in one of the bars near the docks, and knocked her up, and she told him the news a few months later on his next visit, and, well, love, shotgun, whatever.

Carney's pants were already down. Taking his money was the next part — to make it look like a hooker had jumped him in the bushes, along with the empty beer bottles and the spent condoms. Assignation gone wrong. Tale as old as time. But besides the story, the money would help me, too, and I was thankful that he was carrying around what must have been most of his pay packet for that week.

I pocketed the money and tossed the wallet next to his body. I didn't need the ID, just the cash. Then, in the bit of moonlight, I saw the nameplate glinting. Carney. It was the name I had first seen when I was kneeling in Stella Maris.

I leaned down and started to unpin it from the breast of his jacket. For Gus, I figured — not a souvenir, not exactly, but a form of proof. Maybe I could send it to him. But who was I kidding? If there was mail service between the two countries, it went without saying that the envelope would be searched. Bad for Gus. And, well, I had just killed a Polish security officer, and I was going to get away with it if I could get my ass away from the canal without being spotted, and the last thing I needed to be doing was to get caught carrying the nameplate from the dead guy's uniform jacket. Bad for me. Very bad.

I left the nameplate in place, half unpinned. I tossed the shot-put into the canal, and leaned in to wash my hands in the murky water, and then I was gone. Well, after I tossed the guy in the canal, too. Because while, given what I was about to do, I might be able to talk myself out of police trouble three or four times out of 10, me caught carrying an old German revolver would survive approximately zero times out of 10.

The Swinoujscie train station was only about a 10-minute walk, maybe 15 minutes. I looked at my watch, and it was just past 10 p.m. There were still enough people on the streets at 10 p.m. that I wouldn't stand out, and I would be in plenty of time for the slow, stop-at-every-hamlet night train to Szczecin. Nothing against the Poles, but Stettin was a much easier name. The intercity train to Szczecin— the one that the UB was most likely to monitor — took four hours. This one, nine hours. I had checked the schedule when I was killing time in the afternoon. Because, even if I was having trouble admitting it to myself, I really had known all along what I was going to do.

PART III

22

Szczecin wasn't that far on a map. The only reason the train took so long was because it was the mail train. Every dot on the map that had a post office — and that was all of them — paid a clerk to be waiting on what passed for a platform with a sack of envelopes to be passed down the line. There were two cars full of men who sorted what they took in as quickly as they could. The goal was to be done with the last sack by the time they reached the next stop — like, 10 or 15 minutes later. And so, after the first stop, the clerk on the platform handed over his sack and received a sack of sorted mail in return. In the morning, the whole thing happened in reverse.

One of the clerks told me about how it all worked when he was drinking a beer on his break. It was the only interruption I had in nine hours, the only time I wasn't thinking about what I had just done.

Not the killing of Carney. Well, not exactly. I had shaken off the act itself after the first beer, the one I drank in the station in Swinoujscie. That wasn't it. The actions weren't haunting me. It was the decisions.

I hadn't helped Father Pete.

I had killed Carney.

I was going to Krakow.

I was all the way back in.

The whole thing felt a bit out-of-body, but I knew better, deep down. Human being, human decisions. I wasn't kidding myself — well, not completely. Grown man, free will, et cetera. So why did it feel like the bus was driving itself? Why did I feel like a passenger in my own life?

It was a long train ride, a train ride where we must have made 30 stops. I could have gotten off the train at any of them, gotten off and turned my ass around and headed back to Swinoujscie, and then the border, and then Ahlbeck, and then Karin and Lotte. Back to the bar at The Denkler. Back to something resembling a normal life — or, as close to a normal life as I had experienced since 1938. After a dozen years, more, of ducking into the shadows and listening for footsteps behind me and checking the reflections in plate glass storefronts, I had been living a different way — a humbler, simpler, saner way, except for the one-day trips across the border to Stella Maris. If I hadn't found peace, at least I thought I might be able to see it over the next hill. And yet...

I hadn't helped Father Pete.

I had killed Carney.

I was going to Krakow.

I was all the way back in.

I felt terrible about Father Pete, even though I knew it really wasn't my fault. I felt fine about Carney, even though there was no urgent need for me to have bashed in his head with a rock. I was on the train now, first to Szczecin and ultimately to Krakow, even though there wasn't anything I could do to help Father Pete, even though the only certainty waiting for me was the crippling memory of Hyman Pietroski hanging naked in that abandoned building, maybe dead because of me. Felt bad, felt fine, wanted to help, knew I was about to torture myself. Christ. It was like a game of table tennis with the devil, a game using my conscience as the ball.

It truly was pathetic, yet I never got off the train. And even amid all of the old shit that I had stirred up — that I wallowed in and maybe reveled in, if that was somehow possible — there was one image that I couldn't shake: the pier behind me, the little girl running toward me, and the first drips from the melting ice cream cone that were falling on my thumb.

23

After I reached Szczecin, it took three more days of sad-ass local trains before I finally arrived in Krakow. It was a good thing it wasn't four days because then I would have missed Father Pete's meeting with his controller. I wasn't sure how I remembered, but I did. It popped into my mind within minutes of leaving Stella Maris the day I found out he had disappeared. It was at breakfast after I followed Carney to the UB offices. It had been a bit of throwaway color in the story he was telling, but it stuck in my head:

January, April, July, October. Always on the fifth. Always The Steam Whistle café across from the station. Always 5 p.m. Always 5 p.m. on the fifth.

Pete had called the guy "Father X," and I was hopeful that he would be wearing his clerical garb. The alternative would have been me walking up to every man sitting alone and asking, "Father?"

As it turned out, he was wearing his getup but it didn't matter, seeing as how he was the only customer sitting outside, nursing a coffee on a blustery day.

"Father?"

"Yes, yes. Do we know each other?"

"No," I said, then paused, then said, "I'm a friend of Father Pete from Swinoujscie."

In the space of five seconds, his eyes did a transformation from shocked, to suspicious, to alarmed, to placid.

"I'm not sure I know a Father Pete in Swinoujscie," he said.

I sat down without asking. The waiter was nearby and I ordered two more coffees.

"I'm his friend from Germany," I said.

"Again, I'm not sure I—"

"Cut the crap, Father. I mean, I get it. You're worried I'm UB or some such. I'll do my best to convince you before the waiter gets back. Pete was a good man. I was his contact at that end. Once a month, in his confessional at Stella Maris. Shipyard comings and goings, things like that. He had a monsignor, who was a drunk and maybe senile besides, and he didn't trust a nosy substitute priest in his rectory, and he once killed a UB agent who was getting too close. A good man who thought I was going to hell."

"Was?" the priest said.

"Was?"

"You said he was a good man. Are you sure. Was?"

"Not positive, but yeah. I've been around, and I understand how this kind of thing works. Yeah."

"You know, I was hoping, praying," he said. "For fuck's sake — yeah, praying. I'm involved in this business, and I dragged him into it, and now I've been asking the Almighty for... I don't know."

"So you know he's been missing?"

"Yeah, yeah," he said. "They don't report to us — their archbishop is in Szczecin — but because his old uncle is here, yeah, we heard. But I guess I was hoping somehow. It's why I'm. Hoping. Waiting."

The waiter came.

"Third cup," he said. "I won't sleep. Then again, I haven't slept anyway, so..."

He took a sip.

"So, why are you here?" he said.

"I wanted to tell you what I know. I figure I owed him that much."

"Why owed?"

"Look, I feel like shit just like you feel like shit," I said. "I'm going to tell you this — it's not like I'm in confession but, well. I feel bad because he asked for my help and I didn't give it to him. He wanted me to stay in Swinoujscie for a while and, I don't know, watch over him for a bit. But there was no place to stay, and I felt like I needed to get back to Germany — I only came for a day at a time, once a month. And, well..."

"Look, on the feeling-like-shit scale, you'll never beat me. We were in the seminary together, me and Pete. Friends since we were 18. He couldn't believe it when I asked him to get into this, this line of work. He was so naive. He wouldn't have done it for anyone else — I'm pretty sure of that. So, whatever you're feeling... Hell, what's your name?"

"Alex. Alex Kovacs."

"I'm Joe. Joe Krazinski."

"Here's the thing," I said. "He was worried about the substitute priest in the rectory."

"The nosy guy."

"Dabrowski."

"I know the name. He's one of ours. Don't know a lot, but he's one of ours. I've seen his name on paperwork."

I screwed up my face in a question.

"I'm a clerk at the archbishop's office, the chancery," he said. "I guess I see a lot of names. Not always a lot of truth but a lot of names."

Again, I screwed up my face.

"You don't get it, I guess," Krazinski said. "It's all unspoken — there's no way to know who to trust sometimes — but, well, let's just say that both sides of the current political argument are represented in the ranks of the clergy."

"Meaning what?"

"Meaning that in any given parish in Krakow, of the five priests stationed there, one of them probably works with us and one of them probably works with the other side."

I whistled.

"Exactly," he said.

"But aren't you guys supposed to be—"

"Anti-communist?" he said. "Yes. Definitely. Definitely and definitively. Godless communism — yes, that is what we believe. But, you know, the clergy, we're just men like everybody else."

"Except for the sex part."

"Pete told me you were an asshole," Krazinski said, and he smiled. "But he liked you. Anyway, just men. Some can be bought off. Some can be swayed by the perception of power. Some are cowards. Some honestly believe that it's better to go along and get along as they have tanks and mortars and we have pitchforks. So, in every rectory, there's this unspoken knowledge that somebody is working for us and somebody is probably reporting what they hear to the UB."

"Must make for some pretty stilted conversation around the dinner table in the rectory," I said.

"In ours, we talk football. Sometimes we just listen to music while we eat. It's eerie sometimes — but if you're not sure who to trust..."

He sipped the coffee again.

"I want to help you if I can," I said.

"All right, you have to give me two days."

"Why?"

"I'm a clerk in the archbishop's office but I'm not a magician," he said. "But I'll think of something. What's the name in your passport? You have a passport, right?"

I spelled out Kovacs for him.

"What's the nationality?"

"Czech."

"Okay, that can work," he said.

"Work how?"

"Two days," he said. "Same time, 5 p.m., but at a different place. The Grenadier. It's on the other side of the station, across the street. This is the old town side."

He pointed over his right shoulder.

"You want the other side," he said. "But you're going to have to find your own place to stay until then. Have you ever been to Krakow before?"

24

As it turned out, it had not been that hard to soothe Hyman Pietroski when I presented myself as the replacement for the dead kid who had recruited him. Ollie. That was the dead kid's name.

Hyman was nervous as hell, and that was true enough, but he wasn't exactly skittish. There is a difference. His hand actually shook the whole time we were in the bar, and he spilled a bit of his beer on the first two sips, but he wasn't asking out. By the end of the second beer, I had managed to convince him that Ollie's death was nothing more than a drunken tragedy. By the end of the third beer, I almost believe it myself. But, whatever — Hyman had made the commitment, and it seemed as if he was determined to carry on.

We set up a meeting schedule — Thursday nights, 10 p.m. at the empty warehouse in Debniki, on the other side of the Vistula — and Hyman never missed. I hid in the bushes across the street and watched him arrive every time, and it was always on time: 10:00, 10:05, like that. He didn't bring blueprints of the fertilizer factory, not exactly, but copies he was making from memory. As he said, "The major dimensions are accurate but you can't hold me to every last inch of every last compressor. Even they're close, though. And besides, these aren't final, these plans that I'm copying. They'll be tweaked — but only tweaked. Like I said, the major dimensions will stay the same — and they're accurate."

We would chat — I tended to bring a small bottle of something for us to share and tried to calm his nerves. I encouraged him, praised him, lied to him — whatever it took. But there was one truth and I sold it hard: that I had not even the smallest hint of danger on my end; that I didn't sense even a whiff of trouble. That had been true for the first three meetings and it was true for that one, the fourth. I took the three sheets and placed them inside the false lining of my jacket. I left the warehouse and walked back from Debniki, back across the Vistula, and deposited the latest papers in the dead drop — which was the third milk crate in the third of six stacks behind an abandoned dairy. Waiting for me, as always, was the same matchbook from the same restaurant in the old town, Rainbow. The matchbook meant that all was well. In return, I was to leave a matchbook with the papers when Hyman had completed his work and I was heading home to Vienna. I figured there might be two more batches coming based on what Hyman was saying. Two more and out.

Two nights later, I was in The Lamplighter, one of the bars that I rotated through during the week. With only the one meeting per week with Hyman, there was no way I could just stay cooped up in my room the rest of the time. I mean, I had to do something. I was careful enough, not that I really needed to be. Nobody tended to bother much with a guy my age sitting at the bar by himself. I was there with a purpose, and people in bars tended to respect that.

That night, though, that Saturday night, I had mis-calibrated on the vodka, and I really didn't remember a lot at first as I was creeping out of a woman's bed, gathering my underwear and clothes from the floor — and settling for the one sock I managed to find — and creeping out of her apartment.

On the scale of hungover, I felt as if all of the water had been sucked out of my brain but I wasn't close to wanting to throw up. So, *there was that. I regretted the whole thing as soon as I began walking down the apartment staircase and out into the morning. I really regretted it because I couldn't remember even a scintilla of the sex — assuming, of course, that there had been sex.*

And then, as I stood there on the sidewalk and tried to figure out where the hell I was and where my own apartment might be, I sensed it. From my first few steps, I felt as if I was being followed.

It was 7 a.m. on a Sunday, and there were a few people on the streets heading to early Mass. There were enough people going to enough churches — Krakow really was lousy with them, churches — that I couldn't be sure. But, well, intuition. Or, something.

Guy in a black hat, a homburg, and I thought, well, maybe. But only maybe. I went into the next church I came to — there really was one on every street corner, it seemed — Saint Somebody. I sat in the back for a few minutes and left just before Communion. Across the street in a café, two black homburgs. Christ. I really was paranoid.

Still, the rest of that day and all the next, I just felt it. Who was the woman? No idea, just somebody else drinking in the bar. That's what it seemed, anyway. Bits and pieces of it came back after I had sobered up. She was making fun of my passable Polish. She was playing with the loose button on my shirt, making fun of that, too. It all seemed normal enough. Drunk, meet drunk. She was late thirties, I guessed, so age appropriate-ish. If it was a setup, it wasn't obvious. And besides, there was no reason to suspect a setup. There was no reason to believe that anyone in authority knew or cared that I was in Krakow. If they had, they would have busted me already at the warehouse in Debniki, or the dead drop, or my apartment.

Still, the feeling. I couldn't shake it. I felt it all that day and all the next day. I felt it on the whole walk to the next meeting with Hyman on the following Thursday. I did everything I knew to do — "evasive tactics," Fritz called them — and I never saw anybody. Still, the feeling. The fucking feeling. I didn't know. It might have just been guilt. Because of what Fritz always said, always insisted: "Hookers only."

When I met Hyman at the warehouse, I said, "You're being careful, right?"

And he said, "Just as you are, I'm sure. But I'm getting nervous."

"Almost done, right?"

"Yeah, next week. Should be next week. But, I don't know, I just feel like — you see someone look at you funny in the lunch room. One of the bosses, up my ass about this other project that isn't finished. Asks me what's taking so long. Like that. At this point, somebody says 'good morning' and I listen for something suspicious in his tone of voice. I mean, I can't fucking live like that."

"One more week. And as for your boss, well, bosses are bosses. They're not happy unless they're up your ass."

"I guess."

"Trust me," I said, even though I was consumed by the same feelings. The whole walk back, with the papers in the lining of my coat, I felt like throwing up. But there was nothing. The dead drop behind the shuttered dairy was fine. The matchbook was there. I looked around and there was nobody nearby. I listened and heard nothing — well, nothing other than Fritz's voice in my head, yelling about hookers. Really, though, it was fine. Maybe the whole thing was just my imagination. Or, more likely, my guilt.

25

A hotel was out of the question for the same reason that it had been out of the question in Swinoujscie — because there was every reason to believe that the UB was as assiduous about checking hotel registers and the required passport information in Krakow as the Stasi was in Heringsdorf. Which meant I'd be lucky to get through breakfast before the first rap on the hotel room door. The risk was just too great. I mean, I could be red-carded in the first five minutes after kickoff. I couldn't even think about it.

Which meant Moishe.

There was an old synagogue in the Jewish neighborhood, or what was left of it. Not many Jews in Krakow, not then. There was a street that led up to the synagogue with businesses on each side. A florist. A dairy restaurant. A cobbler. A tailor. Moishe Felder was the tailor.

I walked over kind of without thinking, my feet carrying me along the route and my head just following along. Mostly, I was preoccupied with remembering the recognition codes. Because, as it turned out, I had made the decision — without telling Fritz

— to expand the roster of Gehlen operatives in Krakow by one. Moishe was Hyman Pietroski's best friend and confidante. He knew everything anyway, so it wasn't as if it was some great risk when I unofficially deputized him and gave him a code that would tell him I needed help. The code was essentially bullshit — I could just tell him I needed help face-to-face, after all — but it added a layer of authenticity and, hopefully, impressed upon him the seriousness of keeping his mouth shut.

We had only met the one time, and it had been a couple of years. Also, we both were bundled up against the cold the day we met, and I wasn't sure I would recognize him or he would recognize me. When I walked into the door of the tailor shop, and the bell over the door rang, and the voice from the back shouted he was on the way, I didn't know if I recognized it. But when the man appeared, seconds later, it was Moishe. Next to him was a teenage boy.

"I lost my ticket," I said. "It's a brown wool double-breasted with a tear in the lining."

I was pretty sure he recognized me when he came out, but when I said "brown wool double-breasted," I was sure. He turned to the kid, probably his son, and said, "Go on, now. Homework."

"Aye-aye, sir," he said, and then he saluted and said, "Two minutes with the broom and I'm gone."

"Smart ass," Moishe said. And then he looked at me and said, "Kids today." And then, after rifling through a drawer full of tickets, he said, "Your lucky day. I work late tonight. It'll be ready at seven. For your trouble, I'll even deliver it."

I looked at my watch. It was nearly 6. The recognition code came with an understanding of the meeting place: The Gull, one of the dozen or so cafés and restaurants that opened out onto Krakow's massive market square, a place full of people at all hours.

I was waiting with a bottle and two glasses when Moishe sat down. He was out of breath. I stood up, and we hugged, and then I poured him a glass and we drank to Hyman's memory.

"I thought, after…" he said.

"I thought, too."

"What, then?"

"Something that has nothing to do with you that you don't need to know about, that it would be safer if you didn't know about."

"OK, I'm fine with that. I'm out of the business. I mean, I was never in the business, as you know, but I'm out of the business. I mean, really out of the business."

"Good for you."

"I just can't…"

"There's no need to explain. I just need a place to sleep, short term. One or two nights, no more. That's for the other business. But part of why I'm here is Hyman. I'd be lying if I denied it, so I won't. I guess I just need to know more."

"It wasn't your fault, Alex."

"I need to understand it better. I mean, I tell myself it wasn't my fault, but I just can't shake it."

We drank the bottle quickly. The truth was, I had drunk half of it before Moishe got there. It was crap, gut-rot red.

"You can stay with me but you have to be out by Friday," he said.

"What's Friday?"

"My wife and boy will be back. They're at her mother's — she's sick and they're helping out for a few days. And my son, he's there too because, as the smart ass regularly tells me, 'You know, your cooking is for shit.' He thinks I don't know about the girl who lives next door to his grandparents."

"Remember those days?" I said.

"What days?"

"When all you thought about was the girl who lived next door, and the possibilities."

"I wish I could remember that far back," Moishe said.

"Two days, tops," I said.

26

The next morning, Moishe worked for a few hours and then closed the shop.

"A walk," he said.

"Where?"

"It'll help you think," he said.

"How far?"

"I don't know, not bad. Half-hour, maybe less."

I did have a day and a night and a day to kill, so, whatever. We walked from the old Jewish neighborhood and across the Vistula, skirting past the Debniki neighborhood where the abandoned warehouse was, where Hyman Pietroski was hanged. It was easily 15 minutes past that — some houses, some light industry, just shops and shit before it all kind of went away. And then we were there, a big open space with remnants of fencing still in place here and there, like teeth in an old homeless man.

"Płaszów," Moishe said.

I shrugged.

"Our own little concentration camp," he said. "Just for Krakow, mostly — but we got some Czechs and Hungarians, too.

It was more like a way-station, though — although the people they did kill here wouldn't likely appreciate the description. Probably a few thousand, nobody's sure. In the end, they trucked away the ashes and shipped the rest of us to Auschwitz."

"Us? You?"

"If you were in the ghetto in Krakow — and we were all in the ghetto — then this was the next stop," Moishe said.

The foundations of some barracks still existed but the place had been picked clean of anything of value in the years since the war ended. I could only guess where the bricks were now or what roofing holes were being patched by the tarpaper. It was almost like a park — quiet, eerie, the only sounds coming from your breath and from the wind.

We walked for a few minutes and came upon a stone building with a balcony. Moishe said it was called the Grey House, and that it was where the camp commandant lived.

"Goth," he said. "I forget the first name. Sometimes, you would see him in the afternoon, standing on the balcony, surveying his kingdom — but that wasn't the dangerous time. The morning was when you worried. If you were in formation for some kind of inspection, or doing repair work or something, or assembling for outside work — like at that Schindler enamel factory. You've heard of that right?"

"Not really," I said.

"Good man, Schindler. Saved people. Saved friends of mine. But we worked there, or other little factories, or in the quarry over there."

He pointed with his left hand.

"But that was the worry," Moishe said. "The morning, those assemblies. You learned to be very, very afraid when you saw the door of the Grey House swing open and Goth come out. If he was in his full uniform, it was generally not a problem. But if he was wearing his mountain hat — you know, dark green felt with a feather in the brim. What do they call it? Tyrolean? Anyway, if Goth was wearing it, he was out hunting. He'd just fucking shoot whichever Jew was nearby and handy. You saw the hat, you fucking scattered. Even the guards, they didn't punish you for that as long as you didn't run too far. If you just dove in a hole or ducked behind a truck, they were fine with that. I mean, they were all animals, but even the guards knew that the boss was a fucking rabid lunatic."

We walked some more. Moishe pointed out what he thought were the remains of his old barracks — just a pile of broken bricks — but he wasn't positive.

"How long were you here?" I said.

"A couple months. Hyman was here, too, but before me. We'd known each other since we were kids, and we both ended up in Auschwitz, but he was there for over a year. Me, just two months. We saw each other there, too — never talked, but waved. One time. It was just an accident that we saw each other. One time, one wave. It was only after everything that we eventually met again. He came to the tailor shop, just on the off chance. Such a happy day, seeing him again. Great day."

We took a big lap around the grounds. We probably spent an hour there all together. It made me sick, just thinking about it, but the effect on Moishe was different. He had been sad when he pointed out his old barracks and when he pointed out some graves over on a hillside, but that was two minutes out of sixty. The rest of the time, he was matter-of-fact or — and I couldn't believe this — even a bit invigorated. Although that wasn't it, not exactly. Not invigorated but, I don't know, determined. Alive and determined. Me, I just felt like throwing up.

We got back to the gate where we had come in and then retraced our steps back to the tailor shop. Lunch was vegetable soup heated on a hot plate and some rye bread. Moishe rinsed the bowls and then said, "Come on, we're going for a ride."

"You have a car?"

"It's beat to shit but it runs."

"Don't waste your petrol on giving me a sightseeing tour."

"I have a petrol... well... connection," he said.

I raised an eyebrow.

"Don't ask," he said, and then laughed.

"If you say so. But really, connection or no connection, don't waste it on me.

"Not a waste, I promise," Moishe said. "Every Gentile who knows... Not a waste. Trust me on that."

We got into the car and headed east. That much, I could tell. The car did drive rough, and there was a hole in the floorboard on my side, a hole barely patched with cardboard. The car was so loud that the few times we did talk, we were shouting at each other.

The journey was a little less than two hours through farmland interrupted by small villages before we got there. It all seemed entirely unremarkable, the whole trip, until we arrived at the destination: Auschwitz.

When we got there, Moishe shut off the engine but neither of us moved. We sat in the car outside the gate, sat in silence and stared through the windscreen, sat and stared at the gate with "Arbeit Macht Frei" written above it.

"Work sets you free," Moishe said.

I said nothing.

"The joke was on us," he said. "But I wasn't in this part. Most of us weren't. Come on. It's only about five minutes more."

27

I had been to Mauthausen before, the Austrian camp in a quarry. I had seen where they had worked Jews to death and been shocked by the scale. But even that hadn't prepared me for Birkenau.

"It's so—"

"Big, I know," Moishe said.

I caught myself — my mouth was wide open. I thought back to Mauthausen. In my memory, it was the biggest horror I had ever seen. If anything, that image burned into my brain had grown bigger over time. It seemed impossible that anything could top it — in size, in monstrosity. Yet there I was, agape.

"How—"

"I have no idea," Moishe said. "I mean, it's not like I measured. When I was here, I was limited to a pretty small area. But, well, we'll walk to the back — most of the way to the back — and you'll see. I have to think it's more than a mile. Like, easily."

We began to walk and I was mesmerized by what I was seeing in the distance — rows and rows and rows of the remnants of barracks. It was mostly just foundations. A few still had their chimneys, or at least a part. Rows and rows and rows, as far as you could see.

We were walking along some railroad tracks that entered through the front gate and ended at what looked like a platform of sorts.

"Germany efficiency," Moishe said. "You see how the tracks divide the place in two, at least this part? A metaphor, those tracks were. So, the trains came right in here. We called it The Ramp. And we got out with whatever shit we were carrying. They made sure to tell people, 'Take all your belongings, you're going to need them.' They made it out like there was going to be something afterward — some kind of work, some kind of life. Something normal. I was under no illusions — I had been to the other camp, to Plaszow — but when I talked to other people in the camp, especially the Hungarians, they all thought it was a work camp, and they would need their extra clothes and stuff."

He stopped, choked.

"You don't have to," I said.

"I do," he said.

After a long breath, Moishe said, "And there's a guy on the platform, an officer. You get off the train, and you parade by him, and he eyes you up and down, and then he points either to the left or the right. You didn't know what was going on. I went to the right, which meant I got shaved and deloused and a number tattooed on my forearm and a gray striped uniform. The people who went left, we only found out later. Families separated — mama and children to the left, papa to the right. Just wailing and people trying to convince each other that it was going to be all right. Just..."

He didn't finish the thought. He just started walking.

More barracks, rows and rows and rows. As we made our way deeper into the camp, more of the barracks were still standing. They were wooden, rotting. The chimneys were red brick, the ones that were still erect.

"About 400 men slept in each one, give or take," Moishe said. "I counted one time, one day — there was nothing else to do — and, well, 396. Jammed together, it was probably the only way we survived the winter — the stoves didn't heat shit. The bathroom was a couple of big buckets."

We kept walking. It seemed to go on forever. Dozens of barracks. I didn't count, but it had to be a couple of hundred. Row after row after row, divided into sections surrounded by barbed-wire fences. Most of the barbed wire was gone, too, like most of the wood slats on the sides of the barracks and most of the red bricks from the chimneys.

And if I thought I understood the scavengers — free building materials in a flat-on-its-back country after the war, I got it — well, I guess I really didn't. Not after that walk. Because a lot of things in this world are free, but you wouldn't touch them. And how was it possible that you would touch anything from there? If you knew, that is.

I said all of this to Moishe. And all he said was, "If they didn't know, the ones who lived around here, it was because they didn't want to know. You know what I mean? They all say they didn't know. Well, they didn't want to know."

He stopped, thought for a second.

"But, come on," Moishe said. "They knew."

He walked away, muttering.

"They fucking knew," he said, more to himself than to me.

28

"You ever heard of sonderkommando?" Moishe asked.

I shook my head.

"Really? Sonderkommando? Never?"

I shook it again.

"All right," he said. "Hyman, he was a sonderkommando. He sat me down and told me. I mean, I already knew. I was pretty sure, anyway. The one time when we saw each other, well, there was a fence. He was on this side of it and I was on the other side of it. So I knew. But he really felt the need to tell me, to talk about it."

I sat there, mute. Moishe took a deep breath.

"All right, it was like this," he said. "Certain people — after the initial selection up front — certain people were chosen to..."

He stopped. Clearly, he was searching for a word.

"Fuck it," he said. "Certain people were chosen to dispose of the bodies. Sonderkommando. Hyman was a sonderkommando. And when I say chosen, I mean ordered. It wasn't like he had a choice. It wasn't like any of them had a choice."

"Jesus..." I said.

"...was nowhere in sight," he said.

I looked at him, then realized what I had said.

"I'm... I'm sorry."

"Don't be," Moishe said. "I'm just being an asshole. I do sometimes think about how many of those guards went to one of your churches on a Sunday and then burned my people on a Monday, but... fuck it."

He punched my shoulder. In reply, I grabbed a quick handful of the back of his neck.

"So, that's what they did," Moishe said. "The guards, they told the people they were going for a shower, to be deloused. And they stacked up whatever suitcases and shit they'd been carrying, and they got undressed, and they went into the shower rooms, and the guards dropped gas pellets down into the crowd and it killed them."

Stop. Long pause.

"And then the sonderkommando went to work," he said. "Hyman made sure to tell me every last bit of it. They pulled the bodies out. They shaved their heads and saved the hair for whatever. They opened their mouths and pulled the gold teeth and tossed them into buckets. They sorted through the belongings for any valuables and put them into piles. And then they put the bodies into push carts and wheeled them into the crematorium."

Five minutes. Five minutes before Moishe spoke again.

"Hyman said, if the sonderkommando came across a warmer coat than the one they were wearing, they took it. Sometimes they found tins of food or other little trinkets, and sometimes they kept those, too. He said that sometimes they pitched cans of food over the fence, just threw them as far as they could when the guards had their backs turned. Hyman said he liked to think that maybe someone lived for an extra week because of the tin of sardines he threw."

Stop. Another long pause. For some reason, the bit about the sardines produced a tear — which was ridiculous on the face of it. But I guess I just pictured Hyman — my nervous little draftsman, the one who handed me the plans for the fertilizer factory — pitching the tin of sardines over the fence, and it became too real. I mean, I couldn't begin to process the shaving of the heads and the gold teeth and the rest, and I'm not sure my subconscious would even allow the thought to take up residence for long. But the tin of sardines, that stuck somehow, and I cried. I think Moishe saw me flick the tear away.

"Hyman said that the food the sonderkommando ate was better than the rest of us got, which was almost nothing," Moishe said. "He said they were one to a bunk in their barracks, not two or three like the rest of us. But he said, 'We knew it was a death sentence. In the end, they couldn't let us live because we were the only ones who knew.' And he was right. I mean, I was in the same camp and I had no idea. I mean, we suspected — but nobody really knew. I guess we were all hoping that the people who weren't in the bunks with us, that they just got taken somewhere else. It was so many women and children. They couldn't just kill women and children, right? You had to hope, right?"

Hyman told Moishe that there was actually a revolt among the sonderkommando at a certain point. He said he wasn't part of it and only heard about it later when he overheard a couple of the guards talking about it and how they suppressed it.

"'That's when I got sent to No. 4.' That's what Hyman said. Come on, let's walk."

Along the way, he told me about the end. Moishe said the camp was just chaos as the Allies approached — and from where they were, they heard dozens of explosions in the last couple of days. Hyman told him later that it was because they were blowing up the crematoriums, doing their best to destroy the evidence. Hyman told him that the guards wanted to kill the sonderkommando but that some of them, Hyman included, took advantage of the chaos and slipped back in with the regular prisoners.

"That was when we began the walk," Moishe said. "We called it the death march. I ended up nearly in Austria. Hyman was in Czechoslovakia. And the whole way — I remember this so clearly — the guards were asking, 'Were you a sonderkommando? Do you know anybody who was?' That's how worried they still were. That's how important it was that the sonderkommando not survive. I can't imagine how scared Hyman must have been."

After a few more minutes, we arrived at a ruin of a building, the roof caved into the center and the rest in pieces.

"This is No. 4," Moishe said, and then pointed out the general scheme — that's where the Jews went in, that's where they died, that's where the bodies were burned. Point, point, point.

"Hyman made me promise that I'd never forget," he said. "That's why you're here. I'm fulfilling my promise to Hyman."

29

We were walking again, and Moishe pointed to two empty crates near the edge of a small pond.

"Here, sit a minute," he said.

Which we did.

"Now, tell me what you see," he said.

I saw a pond that was the size of a big puddle. You could row a boat across it in fewer than 10 strokes. You could kick a football across it. Okay, maybe I couldn't, but people could. Football people.

"So what do you see?" he asked again.

"I don't know. A little pond."

"You know what I see — what I, what I see every night? I turn off the lights, and I try to get myself settled down, and I come close, and then I think of this place. It's always this place in the end, ever since Hyman told me about it. When I first got out, the thing I saw every night when I closed my eyes was the train tracks and The Ramp. Now, though, it's this. I see this water and I see faces. Thousands of faces, but all kind of blurry. I don't recognize anybody. Hyman took me here, maybe two years after the war — so, really not that long ago — and I think we probably sat on these same crates. And I hear his words, and I see the pond, and I see the blurred faces."

I stayed silent.

"You don't get it, do you?"

"I mean..."

"No, no, I didn't explain," Moishe said. "My fault. I forget what people know and don't know sometimes. My fault. The pond, this right here, is where the sonderkommando dumped the ashes."

I looked at the water again. It was maybe 100 feet from the pile of rubble that used to be the crematorium.

"Hyman said they shoveled the ashes out of the ovens. And then they took those wooden mallets and they crushed the bones that hadn't burned — just bits and pieces, mostly, just hunks of bone that were maybe the size of your fist. Maybe a hip bone, I don't know. They crushed them, and then they walked the wheelbarrows down here, and then they dumped the ashes in."

I couldn't imagine. The whole thing was so big and so monstrous as to be overwhelming. It drowned your senses, the relentless horror that the place represented. Now this. I might never look at a pond or a lake in the same way again. I might not be able to look at any body of water without thinking of wheelbarrows full of ashes.

"I can't tell you how guilty he was," Moishe said. "It was crazy, and I told him it was crazy — once, twice, a dozen times. But he couldn't shake it. He would say, 'But they were my people.' And I would say, 'But you didn't kill them.' And he would say, 'I might just as well have.'

"He really didn't want people to know. When we found out they existed, the sonderkommando, it was just one more layer of horror heaped on the rest of it. I don't know anybody who held any of it against any of them. The survivors from the camps, they knew what kind of hell it was. Like I said, I don't personally know anybody who resented the sonderkommando. Fuck, I felt terrible for my friend, for what he had to do, and I think most people felt the same way."

"Not everybody, though?" I said.

"Nobody I knew, nobody he knew."

"But not everybody?"

"No, not everybody," Moishe said. "Part of me, I guess I understand. I mean, some people are just so damaged and, well, they want to think the sonderkommando were collaborating, that they were eating filet mignon and stealing rings and jewels. So there are a few. They've been in the newspapers, complaining — but, really, just a few. Nobody I know. Nobody Hyman knew. But every one of them, for Hyman, was an arrow in his heart."

Moishe looked at me. Now he was crying.

"He was always talking about the shame he felt. Just endless, pointless conversations — and if he was drinking, oh man. And it was always the same. I always told him he didn't have a choice. And Hyman always said, 'I did, though. I could have chosen to die.' And I would say, 'You made the same choice everybody in that camp would have made, the choice to live as long as you could.' And he would just mutter, 'I could have chosen to die.'"

Moishe stopped, wiped his face with his sleeve.

"Fuck it, let's go home," he said.

We stood up, and that's when the shot rang out.

30

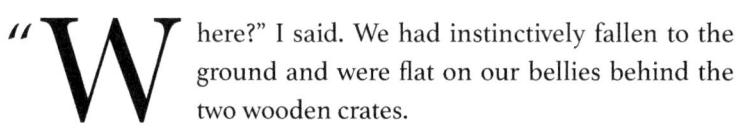

"Where?" I said. We had instinctively fallen to the ground and were flat on our bellies behind the two wooden crates.

Moishe didn't answer.

"Where?" I said. "Where did it come from?"

Moishe gestured with a flick of his nose. He was indicating a line of trees even deeper into the camp than we were, even farther from The Ramp and the front gate.

"What's back there?"

"Woods," he said. "Don't know how deep. I assume there's a town of some kind on the other side, or farms, or something, but I really don't know. I don't even know if there's a fence — and even if there was back when we were here, would there still be a fence? If so many of the posts and the wire were taken from in here, I mean, how much would have survived back there? So, I have no idea. But even if there was a fence, hell, it's not like there are guards or anything."

So we were lying there, in a death camp, absorbing gunfire. The irony. I thought of it immediately but I didn't want to bring it up to Moishe. You survive the ghetto in Krakow, and the camp in Plaszow, and then Auschwitz — and then you take a bullet because you had promised your dead friend to do everything you could to keep the memory of the place alive?

"You're not hit?" I said.

"No, fine. Fine. You?"

"I'm fine."

"So, what the fuck?"

"That's the question," I said.

I moved slightly to my left to see if I could see anything. It was early evening, dusk-to-dark. Closer to dark but not quite there. I moved just a few inches, and then a few inches more, and then another shot — a loud crack into the stillness. I stopped moving to my left. I wasn't the type who touched a hot stove twice.

"Well, at least we know we're on the proper side of the crates," I said.

Pinned down, we spoke in whispers. We were going to have to make a move at some point — some point soon — and take a chance. For all we knew, the rifle — or rifles — were advancing on us as we lay there. Every second we stayed hidden behind the crates increased the risk. I knew that intuitively.

Still, we thought. We couldn't help but think. Why?

The conversation between the two of us was in whispers. It was a reflex but, well, why? It wasn't like the rifle or rifles didn't know where we were. We were protected by the crates but we weren't hiding. Not from the gunfire, anyway. Maybe from our fears, but not from the gunfire.

Still, we whispered and we traded theories for maybe two minutes. Maybe less. I started.

"Maybe someone saw me at the tailor shop. Maybe they decided they didn't like us meeting up again."

"But I'm just a tailor. I mean, I never did anything."

"You're just a tailor, but I'm not."

"I don't know," Moishe said. "I mean, a shot in the fucking night? The UB would just arrest you and do it that way. They could have grabbed you at the tailor shop. If they knew we were here, they could have just waited by the car—"

His theory made some sense to me — this was a pretty elaborate bit of business for the UB and, as Moishe said, there were easier alternatives. Driving way out to Auschwitz, to the ass end of nowhere — no, Moishe was right. This wasn't the UB.

His dissertation, though, was interrupted by another rifle shot. This one was directed at him, and it caught the edge of the wooden crate and produced a small shower of wood chips.

"Oh, fuck — we're sitting ducks," he said.

"I know. I know. So, what's your other theory? I mean, is there something valuable back here? Or in here? Something that you know of?"

Moishe took a beat.

"What's valuable in here? Only the memories," he said.

"But shooting?"

With that, another rifle shot cracked. It didn't hit anything. I felt like it whizzed over my head but I wasn't sure. It might have been my nerves. Or, my imagination.

"God. What the hell?"

"The memories," Moishe said. "It's the memories. They deny it, still. They don't want people to know. They were so worried about the sonderkommando like Hyman, surviving and telling what they did. I mean, they blew up the place before they left. You saw it, and you'll never forget it. And, shit. They don't want that. They want to act like it never happened."

"They?" I said. "The war's over for five years. They? Still?"

"Don't be naive," Moishe said. "You're too fucking smart for that."

The truth was, I wasn't naive. I knew the Nazis were not dead, not nearly. Since the end of the war, I had seen them in places as varied as Istanbul and Helsinki. I had seen them in the Gehlen Org. Not dead. Very much not dead. Camouflaged, showered and shaved and perfumed — yes. But not dead. Very much not dead.

One more rifle shot — this one hitting my crate — and I was ready for us to make our move. But here was the calculus, based on nothing but intuition. There was no question in my mind that the rifle would come closer as it got darker — and then we were screwed, as in dead. The rifle had no fear because we hadn't fired back. The rifle — or, rifles — would come closer. But moving at that moment involved its own risk for us because there was still a bit of daylight. Not much, just a tiny bit, but some. Gloaming-like.

"What do you think?" Moishe said.

"I think now," I said. "On our bellies. Just crawling. Don't pick up your head, not even an inch. The grass is dark, our clothes are dark, we have a chance here. I think we have a decent chance."

"God. Decent?"

"Best I can do. No guarantees in this life. Hell, you know that better than anybody. So, look. The barracks over there."

I pointed to my left. It was maybe 200 feet away and looked like it couldn't survive a strong wind, except for the chimney. But it was still standing, and if we got to the far side, it would be between us and the source of the rifle fire.

"Just don't lift your fucking head, not an inch," I said.

It probably took us 10 minutes to crawl the 200 feet, but it worked. No shots, nothing. Along the way, after the grass, there was bare dirt for maybe the last 25 feet. My nose was full of it, but I didn't dare lift my head. When we reached the barracks, both of us looked like coal miners — but we were there. And after a minute of wiping our faces and blowing our noses into our hands, as quietly but as forcefully as we could, the two of us regained our breath.

"From here, I think we just have to run for it," I said.

It was a little darker, but neither of us dared to look around the barracks to see if the rifle or rifles were advancing. Hot stoves and all that.

"If we sit — well, we're sitting ducks," I said. "They knew where we were, and they can see as well as we could see that this was the closest thing to hide behind. I think we have to chance it again. Can you run?"

He took a deep breath and said, "Sure."

"You saw how far it is to the car. Like, maybe a mile."

Moishe nodded. Then he took another deep breath, and I was worried. I mean, it wasn't like I was Paavo Nurmi or anything but I could run a mile. Moishe, on the other hand, was a tailor who sat on his ass all day and mended the cuffs on pants. But, what was our choice?

"When we run, we should weave a little," I said.

"Weave?"

"Like, just not in a straight line. Harder to aim if you're moving a little left to right and then right to left."

"You're making that up."

"So fucking sue me," I said. "But it makes sense, no?"

Two more deep breaths for each of us.

"All right, let's go," I said.

And with that, we ran. Moishe did fine, as it turned out. Why I would question his determination? Well, it spoke to my naivete. I was standing in a death camp, and I knew he had survived hell, yet I thought in my head that he might not be able to run a mile with rifles potentially chasing him? What kind of fool was I?

There was only one more shot, maybe 10 seconds after we started. Just one more crack, and it hit neither of us. The two of us almost fell when we heard it, but we both kind of reached out to each other and righted ourselves — and that was it. After that, all I could hear was my labored breathing. Heaving, struggling — past the rows and rows of barracks, and then The Ramp, and then along the train tracks that came in through the front gate. When we got there, Moishe collapsed into the driver's seat while I threw up behind the car.

And then, as we pulled away, there was one final shot. Missed again.

31

I left Moishe to his work the next morning and headed out. Neither of us had any idea who was firing at us, not really. Seeing as how the UB hadn't knocked on the door in the middle of the night pretty much ruled them out. And if the Nazi idea made the most sense, it left us no closer to actual identities. We both realized that without saying it. The truth was, we said very little. My goodbye consisted of "thanks" and a hug.

"Keep in touch," he said.

"You don't mean that."

"No, I do. Well, kind of."

Just to be sure, we set up a weekly check-in at our place on the main square, The Gull. That is, if either of us felt the need to check in. Whoever got there first would take an outside table. Whoever got there second would only stop if he felt it was important to talk. Short of that, he was to keep walking.

"And it has to be important — like, really important," I said.

"Like life or death."

"Or life and limb," I said.

I wandered the streets until my meeting with Father Joe Krazinski at 5 p.m. Just to make sure, around noon, I found The

Grenadier. It was where Krazinski said it would be, on the other side of the train station. After that, I just walked around the old town that was so much better preserved than most. It still amazed me that the war never really came here because it had come, and come hard, to so many other places. Geography, whim, who knew? Some places had been flattened and, five-plus years later, were still pancakes. But Krakow? Poorer than it had been, sure, but classic and charming and entirely intact — and I had no idea why.

At five, Krazinski was waiting for me at an outside table. He wasn't wearing his priest getup. Instead, he had on black pants, a blue striped shirt and a dark gray jacket. On the chair next to him was a small parcel wrapped in brown paper, like it had come from a laundry.

"What's that?" I said.

"And hello to you, too."

"Seriously."

"A cassock, collar, black shirt and black pants," Krazinski said. He bent over and looked beneath the table.

"Good, black shoes," he said. "You would have to go buy a pair otherwise. I think I pretty well guessed your sizes but there was no way I could guess the shoes."

"What are you talking about?"

"Here," he said. The priest reached into his jacket pocket and produced two bits of paperwork. As I read them, I could see that they allowed for the presence of a Father Alex Kovacs, of Czech nationality, in the Archdiocese of Krakow for a period of one month to attend a philosophy seminar at Jagiellonian University and to assist at the Church of St. Anne.

"It gives you a legal purpose for being here and a place to lay your head," Krazinski said. "Best I can do on short notice. Just carry the paperwork with you at all times. Even if the UB did become aware of you — and they very well might — this should carry you through. If you look at it, it's got a border stamp from two days ago. It's pretty legit."

"Pretty?"

"Very legit. We have an actual stamp that was lifted by a friend. It's not a fake. You'll be fine."

"You sound like you're trying to convince yourself more than you're trying to convince me."

"It's legit, I promise."

I asked a little about the cassock and the collar, and Krazinski promised I could figure it out. Besides, he said, nobody would look twice. He said, "In Krakow, somebody in a cassock, he's invisible unless he's in a whorehouse. On the streets, though, nobody even looks at your face. All they see is the black."

As for the Church of St. Anne, my residence, Krazinski said that the pastor was in on the scheme, and that I would be able to come and go.

"What about the other priests in the rectory? There are other priests, right?"

"There are. Don't worry."

"Easy for you to say."

Krazinski started to say something, then stopped himself.

"Oh, and your shady priest from Swinoujscie? Your Father Dabrowski? He's stationed at St. Andrew's."

"Where's that?"

"On Grodzka, just up the hill from the castle. Fifteen minutes from here. Twenty if you walk slow."

I knew the vague area. I mean, I knew where the castle was. Grodzka. I repeated it a couple of times so I would remember.

"Shorter than you, younger than you," Krazinski said. "Light hair. Biggish nose."

"St. Andrew's?" I said.

"A little church. Really little. You'll see."

"And how did he get transferred to Swinoujscie and then transferred back?"

"Well, there's paperwork," he said. "I found it. It was misfiled, likely on purpose. Certainly on purpose. But I dug it up and got the name of the auxiliary bishop who signed it. Very helpful information, that. I have to thank you. It fills in a piece of our puzzle."

"About who's working for who?"

Krazinski nodded. He had been drinking a coffee when I arrived, and the waiter had never come over when I sat down. He finally did, and we switched to beers. I didn't really have much to say as we sipped, but it seemed that Krazinski did.

"You going to spit it out or what?"

"The beer?"

"Cute."

He sipped again.

"All right. We were hoping..."

"We?"

"I have superiors," the priest said.

"To which of your affiliations are you referring?"

He shrugged.

"Your official job or your extracurricular activities? Which of your superiors?"

"In this case, both."

"Okay, then. And your superiors were hoping..."

"That you would take care of Father Dabrowski."

"Take care of, as in..."

He held up his hands.

"You're fucking kidding me, right?"

"Do I sound like I'm fucking kidding you?"

"The holy Catholic Church wants me to..."

He held up his hands again.

"Can't you just transfer him somewhere? I mean, I don't

know who you think I am, or what I do for a living, but I'm not a hired gun. I'm not an assassin."

"I've delivered the message."

"You haven't said shit."

"I've said plenty, and you've understood every word of it," the priest said. And then he got up and left, half of his beer undrunk and the bill suddenly mine. Priests were good at a lot of things, but especially the walking-out-on-the-check part.

32

I sat on a bench behind St. Anne's, my new home, and watched the side door for an hour or two before entering. Force of habit — and besides, I needed time to think. It was an odd place, the bench where I was sitting, a riot for the senses. The church backed up onto one of Krakow's zillion public parks, this one called The Palace of the Fine Arts garden. The green hit you, and so did the shadows created by the canopy of trees that covered the path. What the trees were, I had no idea. I must have slept through that chapter in school. Oaks, maples, whatever — big and tall and full enough that only shafts of sunlight got through in an irregular pattern. So it was green, and it was cool, and there was one more of the senses that was tickled, too. It was loud — not from the old men sitting on the benches along the path, but from the pigeons that were everywhere around the bread that the old men were tossing and then nowhere as a walking human approached. The birds created a true racket. I guess the trees kept the sound from escaping.

Amid all of that, I sat and thought. I had rules when I started, one rule in particular: that I only killed people in self-defense. My life had to be in danger — my life, or the life of a comrade, or the life of an innocent. That was the rule. Was, I guess.

The major amendment, one that had been ratified unanimously by my conscience after the first time, was that besides self-defense, I was permitted to kill people who deserved to be killed. People who had harmed comrades or innocents, or who had the potential to harm them. It made me judge, jury and executioner, and I understood that. It was not a burden that I took lightly. In the handful of cases when it came into play, I was confident in what I was doing — both at the time and after a thorough examination of my aforementioned conscience.

Like with Carney the previous week. He was just evil. It was obvious when Gus Braun first told me the story about his wife and daughter, and it was obvious when Carney was reveling in the memory even as I held a gun to him along the canal side. Evil, unquestionably — and I was fine with what I did. I slept fine. More than fine.

But this Father Dabrowski — I was less sure about him. Judge, jury, executioner — and I just didn't know. I mean, I knew that Father Pete had been worried about Dabrowski, and I now had a sense that Dabrowski was playing for Team UB against Father Krazinski and Team Good Guys. It was crazy when you thought about it, how they all had taken the same vows and that so many of them had ended up on opposite sides of such an existential question. Or maybe it wasn't existential. Maybe it was just about power and influence and greed and envy and all of those human things.

Anyway, I did have a sense, yes. But I had nothing resembling proof that Dabrowski had informed on Father Pete, and that his report to the UB had begun the chain of events that led to Father Pete being very much disappeared — and, almost certainly, very much dead. After all, Father Pete had already tangled with a UB officer, and the officer had ended up in the canal after the untangling. That could have been what got Pete snatched. Really, it was more likely that it was Dabrowski, if I really thought about it.

And, well, I was not an assassin. I was not a hired gun. I did not kill people for sport or for money. And as judge, jury and executioner, I didn't have enough on Dabrowski. Maybe some time, maybe soon. But as I sat in the back row of the tiny church that was St. Andrew's, I wasn't convinced. Not enough to kill the guy saying Mass on the altar.

I was in my civilian clothes as I sat here, and stood there, and knelt there. I couldn't believe how small the church was inside. I mean, I felt like I could reach out and grab Dabrowski as I stood there. St. Andrew's was right next to Sts. Peter and Paul, a much bigger church, but still. It was so narrow inside, and there were only about eight or nine rows on either side of a middle aisle, and each row seated only two people comfortably, and that was provided one of them wasn't even mildly overweight. It was a beautiful church, a gold-clad jewel, but so small. Tiny, even. And why it even existed baffled me, what with the big church right next door.

That morning, there were 18 people at the 7 a.m. Mass. And even though his back was to me most of the time, facing the altar, I knew the priest was Dabrowski. The nose was unmistakable every time he turned his head.

He didn't preach, not like a Sunday Mass, so I didn't get any sense of his personality. He was, like most priests on weekdays, moving swiftly through the prayers so that the people in the seats could get to work. And I left just before Communion. I didn't need to be going up to the altar rail. There was no sense getting that close. For all I knew, Dabrowski had seen me before when I was talking to Father Pete. There was no upside in testing that hypothesis.

I saw a café across the cobbled street and waited at a table outside with a newspaper and a coffee. It was really shit coffee, a universal problem in post-war Europe. I mean, before the second war, I had grown to adulthood in Vienna. I knew good coffee, at least in my memory. I also knew bad coffee, but this was a rung below. Even so, I ordered two cups while I read the paper and waited.

In the half-hour after the Mass ended, I watched two other priests leave out of the same nondescript door that was to the left of the church's ornate main entrance. That had to be the way in and out of the residences. I ordered the second coffee and was just finishing it when the door opened again. It was Dabrowski.

I wasn't going to follow him. I had a month, after all, and the odds he was going to be involved in anything nefarious at 8 a.m. were relatively low. No need to rush things, I figured. But then I couldn't help myself. I mean, what if he was headed to UB headquarters for some kind of debriefing or to receive instructions for whatever was next? It was a possibility, I guessed. Of course, I had no idea where the local UB headquarters was. And if he met a guy in a dark suit for coffee, there would be no way for me to know if it was his UB handler or just some parishioner who wanted to open up about his sick wife. But, like I said, I couldn't help myself.

So I left some coins for the waiter and began walking. The sidewalks were hectic with men headed for work, and I was more than a block behind, and there were periods — like, say, 10 seconds here and there — when I thought I had lost him only to see him reappear. Finally, after 10 minutes and a couple of rights and lefts, he climbed some steps. It was a school — a pretty big school. That must have been Dabrowski's day job — religion teacher, math teacher, chaplain, whatever. So I learned something, but I guess I really learned nothing.

33

Two nights later. Same café. Black jacket and a hat this time, rather than the blue jumper and the bare head and the black eyeglasses the first time. A small plate of pierogis and fried onions in front of me along with a glass of wretched red wine. Not as bad as the coffee, the wine, but still terrible.

I was sitting, waiting, watching the little side door next to the main entrance at St. Andrew's. I had a paperback novel with me, and I did my best to get through it — my Polish was improving, if nothing else, and I could guess most of the words I didn't know from their context. I had been tempted to ask the waiter for the occasional bit of help, but that was stupid. There was no sense identifying myself as a foreigner, even if he could probably tell from my accent that Polish wasn't my native tongue. For all he knew, I had lived in Krakow for decades — not a Pole by birth, certainly, but maybe by marriage.

I was sitting there, eating and drinking and reading and, really, just guessing. Father Pete had mentioned that Dabrowski went out for drinks sometimes, and it was Friday night, and, well, whatever. A guess. A hunch. And nothing better to do, anyway.

Just after 7 p.m. the door opened and Dabrowski came out. I somehow managed to get the waiter's attention and pay him quickly, but by the time I was on my feet, Dabrowski must have been two blocks ahead. I could see him, just barely, and I hustled without running. I even looked at my watch one time in case anybody thought my speed to be odd. Late for a restaurant reservation, or a date, or something.

I slowed down, back to normal pace, when I was about a half-block behind the priest and his big nose. The sidewalks were active — Friday night and all that — and there was a steady line of people headed to the main square in the old town, the massive space ringed on all four sides by restaurants and cafés. There were enough people — mostly couples, all ages, out for a meal or a drink — that I wasn't the least bit worried that Dabrowski would notice me. A half-block buffer was fine. Honestly, 100 feet would have been fine.

We got to the square and it was teeming with all manner of humanity — old couples holding hands while strolling aimlessly, mothers and fathers herding small children, packs of young men whistling at packs of young women who sneered in reply. Life.

But Dabrowski knifed through the chaos, navigating the cross-currents of people in the enormous square, striding past the restaurants and the cafés. Striding with a purpose. On the far side of the square, through the maelstrom, he entered one of the feeder streets and, in the next block, stopped at a door, looked around briefly, and then entered. Above the door was a sign that was actually more like a marquee, lit and gaudy and orange. One word glowed, the name of the place: Feniks.

I gave him five minutes, taking a half-lap around the main square, and then followed Dabrowski inside. The entrance was an empty space with a staircase. One level down and you were in the place. Feniks. It must have been Polish for "tacky, schlocky shit."

It was all one room, a big space. Other than tacky, schlocky, and shit, the first word that came to mind was shiny. Lots of light. Glass. Chrome. It was, I supposed, the modern Commie vision of the future. There was a bar on one side, and tables — twos and fours — arrayed around the other three sides. In the middle was a dance floor. In one corner was a three-piece combo playing music I did not recognize. Commie dance tunes of some kind, I presumed. Artie Shaw, it wasn't.

I asked for a table for two. The hostess, in a slinky red ball gown, arched her eyebrow and said, "A date?"

"That's the plan," I said.

"A plan set in concrete?" she said. Another eyebrow arch.

"Wet cement, actually, but I'm hopeful," I said.

I met her arch with a weak smile. She patted my hand and smiled in return, then led me to the table. All a part of the service, I assumed.

It took a minute for my eyes to adjust. The dance floor was well lit, but the tables were in relative darkness — not dark-dark, but enough that it took a second to focus. It was only after I ordered a drink — vodka with a beer chaser — that I scanned the other tables around the perimeter and spotted Father Dabrowski and his big nose. He was almost directly opposite me on the far wall at a table for two.

The priest's companion was a man, forty-ish, similar to Dabrowski. He had wild hair, a bird's nest of an arrangement. I was too far away to hear anything, even if the band hadn't been playing. I was too far to really get a good look, beyond the bird's nest, and that didn't even take into account the couples dancing in and out of my line of sight.

I did my best not to stare and I'm sure I succeeded. The angle was fine for me to take the occasional casual glance. Based on the way the two of them appeared to laugh during the conversation, they were clearly friends. It wasn't a business meeting. There was also a lot of arm patting and fake punches to the shoulder and the like. Definitely friends.

Now, was it possible to be friends with your UB controller? Sure, possible, but definitely not encouraged in the secret police recruitment manual. I mean, I assumed there was such a book that guided UB officers in how to act with their sources, and I assumed that buddy-buddy, cuff-the-guy-around-the-neck behavior in a busy nightclub wasn't anywhere in the table of contents. I had to think that if the UB was like the rest of its brethren — all the bastard children of the Gestapo and the NKVD — that fear was in the title of every chapter of the book. Types of Fear. Creating the Fearful Environment. Employing Fear. When Fears Come True.

Playful pats on the shoulder? Not so much.

Friends, then. Dabrowski had friends. Maybe two priests in civilian clothing out for an evening in a nightclub, an evening of pretending they hadn't taken those pesky vows. There was no way to know, though. Two hours and four vodka-and-beers later, the two of them got up to leave. I followed maybe a minute behind them — I had to accept the condolences of the hostess in the slinky red ball gown.

"So sorry about your date," she said.

"No worries. Nothing lost, nothing gained."

"Well done, chin up. Your wet cement will harden soon enough."

She winked. I honestly thought about staying, but only for about a second. I had a priest with a big nose to follow. My hardening would have to wait. And as it turned out, the big nose and the wild hair split up on the street, and Dabrowski headed straight back to St. Andrew's.

34

I took the long way around the perimeter of the main square, just to make sure I wasn't being followed. I hadn't sensed anything on this trip to Krakow — not leaving my temporary home at St. Anne's in the full priestly getup most mornings and heading in the direction of Jagiellonian University for my imaginary seminar, not the other times when I wandered around in civilian clothes.

Even with my purposeful meandering, I was still a half-hour early to The Gull. There was no reason to think that anything was up. I was just following through on what I had told Moishe. I was more than confident that the UB had no idea who he was, and that no one could make a connection between the two of us, but still. If it made him feel better to know that I was available if he got even a whiff of danger, well, then it would make me feel better.

I was on my second glass of wine about 10 minutes later when I saw Moishe approaching in the distance. When he closed to within about a hundred feet, I turned my head slightly and actively avoided looking at him — turned my head, looked at my watch, craned my head in the other direction as if searching for the waiter. Who, as it turns out, I managed to make eye contact with.

And then Moishe fucking sat down.

"Jesus," I said.

"No, no."

"What do you mean, 'no, no?'"

"It's not an emergency," he said.

"Then why the hell did you stop?"

"I have something to tell you."

"Are you sure you weren't followed?"

"I made two deliveries before this," Moishe said. "I'm sure. Just get me a drink."

We didn't say anything as we waited for the waiter to bring two more wines. After he brought them, and we each took a slug, I looked at him and shrugged.

"Something I meant to tell you before," Moishe said.

"So you said."

"It's about Hyman."

I waited. Shrugged again.

"It's just," Moishe said, and then he stopped.

"Spit it out."

"It's just that I always thought he was going to hang himself in the end," he said.

"Just suicide?"

Moishe nodded. His eyes dropped.

"It doesn't make any sense," I said. "I mean, think about his life — just from what you told me. He survived things that, God... Those camps. And the sonderkommando. I mean, God. He survived that, why would he kill himself?"

"Are you hearing yourself?" Moishe said. "How much of his soul was taken along the way? How much did the memories weigh on him? How much mental energy did it take for his mind to clear after he turned off the lights at night? And then, the stress of what he was doing for you..."

He stopped, drank.

"But that's the thing," I said. "Look, I'm no saint here but I didn't recruit him. But when I came, he could have gotten out of it. I was prepared to try to charm him into staying, but it really didn't take much charming on my part. He was committed to the task. I'd like to think it might have given him a purpose. You know, a reason to keep going. Something different to think about when the lights were out. Something good. Something he was accomplishing. Something for good."

We both sat for a minute and drank. I hadn't preplanned that little speech — it just kind of tumbled out — but it kind of made sense. And if I was trying to make myself feel better in the process, well, I would have liked to believe what I was saying. That Hyman was doing good and that he would recognize as much.

"Besides," I said. "I told you about how I found him."

"Yeah, hanged."

"Yeah, hanged. But what about the bruises? What about the pinky? What about the burns on his nipple? That was done to him — it's obvious. Not self-inflicted. No way."

I made eye contact with the waiter. Two more.

And then, Moishe said, "Well, there's another thing I didn't tell you before. It's the other reason I'm here."

I looked at him and waited.

"Well, there was a woman," he said.

35

It should have been about a 10-minute walk, but I made Moishe turn it into a half-hour of extraneous lefts and rights and doubling-back. We talked as we walked, and he filled in the details.

"Hyman didn't think I knew, but I did," he said.

"About the woman? How? Caught him sniffing his fingers?"

"What are you, 16?"

"So, how? You saw them together?"

"No. I've never seen her, actually. Let's just say he was metaphorically sniffing his fingers."

"Metaphorical sniffing or metaphorical fingers?"

"You really are an asshole," Moishe said. "Look, I've known him forever. I could just tell. And he admitted it when I asked him, even as he swore me to secrecy. He didn't want anybody to know."

We walked and made our lefts and rights, and I did all of the basic spy stuff — stopping and checking the reflections in the plate glass window of a furniture store, stopping again and tying my shoe and trying to see if somebody behind us stopped short and began some sudden window shopping of his own. Nothing, though.

"But why?" I said.

"Why what?"

"Why didn't he want anybody to know about his girlfriend? I mean, I'm sure his friends would be happy for him, and as for everybody else, they wouldn't give a shit either way. Everybody's in their own head most of the time, so busy with their own crap that they're too preoccupied to worry about anybody else's. So, why?"

"I actually said just about exactly those words to him once," Moishe said. "But, well, you had to know Hyman."

"I did know him, remember? At least a little."

"Yeah, a little," he said. "But really only a little. You saw a guy who was pretty nervous about doing a pretty brave thing. But that was only one compartment of his life. Just the present. For Hyman, though, the past hung there like a lead-weighted cape that he could never shake off."

We were passing one of the million little pocket parks in Krakow, and Moishe took a seat on an empty bench.

"If you really knew him, it'd be easier for you to understand," he said. "But, just, well, put it like this. He was so grateful for her, I'm sure, so happy and grateful that she was in his life that he didn't want her to be tainted in any way."

"Tainted?" I said. "How?"

"The sonderkommando."

"For fuck's sake..."

"I know," Moishe said. "I know and I agree. But that's what he thought, that him being in the sonderkommando would taint her. We already talked about this. For some, I guess, maybe he would have been right. But it was only some. Like I told you, almost none. Most of us, most everybody who had been in that camp, we understood. We had lived through hell and we understood. I mean, it was fucking hell. Just..."

Moishe stopped. He waved his hand in the air as if he was swatting at an imaginary fly. It was almost pathetic, a lifeless wave, hopeless.

"Just fucking hell," he said. "We were all handed a fate by the Nazis, and then it was up to God somehow. Whether you died on the day you got off the train, or you survived for a week, or a month, or six months, or if you were a sonderkommando — you had nothing to do with it, not with the timing or the circumstances. Nothing to do with it. No control over the circumstances of the outcome. If you were there, you understood. I told Hyman that a thousand times. I told him that we understood."

We sat on the bench for another minute and watched exactly two people walk past us in that time. We were a little farther out, away from the main square, and it was quiet.

"It's just that block there," Moishe said. He pointed to his right. "Second house on the left. Second house, second floor. The name on the mailbox is Lefkowitz. Sophie Lefkowitz. I've seen it walking by. Come on, let's go."

"You're not going," I said.

"The hell I'm not."

"You're not going. Period."

"Little spinster too dangerous for me? The hell with that."

"The little spinster, no," I said. "But the people who might be watching the little spinster, maybe. You ever thought of that? I don't know how big the UB is here in Poland, but if it's anything like the Stasi in East Germany, this city is crawling with informers. So, if the UB had anything to do with killing Hyman, well, they might still be watching her — maybe just the neighbor across the hall keeping an eye out. Something as simple as that. You don't need that kind of attention — trust me. You're clean now, as far as we know, and we need to keep it that way. I can't have it on my conscience. I can't have both you and Hyman."

"Hyman wasn't your fault," Moishe said. "I'm telling you, I really thought he might kill himself."

"I told you, the evidence doesn't point to that if you look at all of it."

"Says you."

"Yes, says me," I said. "Now look — I appreciate what you're saying. There are days when I even believe it. This isn't one of them, though. And now I'm going to cross the street and knock on Sophie Lefkowitz's apartment door. And I'm going to tell you, with all the affection I can muster, that it's time for you to get the fuck out of here."

"Wow, I'm touched," Moishe said.

"Just fucking go."

"All right, all right," he said. Then, he turned on his heel and walked away without another word. A minute later, I walked past the mailbox that said "Lefkowitz, S." and climbed to the second floor. Hers was the front apartment. I knocked, and she answered quickly. Maybe she had watched me enter the building through her window.

I introduced myself and waited. I didn't mention Hyman. I just said my name and stood there, shifting my weight from one foot to the next. It took her a second but then it registered. It wasn't like in the cartoons, when a light bulb appeared over some character's head. Instead, the light was in her eyes.

"Alex Kovacs," she said. "Yes, please come in."

36

Tea was brewed. Little pastries were produced. I took one sip and one bite. Neither of us said a word.

"I miss him," Sophie said.

"So do I."

"Why are you here?"

"Not sure."

"Please, Alex. What do they say in the American movies? Don't kid a kidder. Why are you here?"

I stopped, sipped, and chewed, stalling as I tried to come up with the right words. It was futile, that search. I was trying to be nice to Sophie, compassionate, but my head was full of my own shit and that was what dominated. I was there in that apartment for me, not her, and that was the honest truth. I was there because I was worried that I had gotten Hyman killed because of the lingering suspicion that I had been followed out of that woman's apartment after that drunken night — that my carelessness had gotten Hyman killed somehow. I was hoping to salve my conscience and I was using her. Unvarnished reality, then.

Anyway, I ended up blurting out a bunch of stuff that ended

with, "But really, I guess I just wanted to tell you that I think his death might be more complicated than you believe, and that I think it might be my fault. I mean, I don't think he killed himself."

"That's fine," Sophie said. "But I know for a fact that he killed himself."

That knocked me back — like, literally, deeper into the cushions of the chair.

"How could you know?"

"Because Hyman told me he was going to kill himself," she said. "The night before, we lay in bed all night and he told me why, and I tried to talk him out of it."

She stopped, and produced a handkerchief from a pocket in the front of her housecoat, and wiped her eyes.

"I thought I had talked him out of it, too," Sophie said. "We slept for maybe an hour, and when he woke up to go to work, he said, 'I feel better. I'll see you tonight.'"

She stopped again, blew her nose.

"Last words," she said. "'I'll see you tonight.'"

She sipped the tea and made a face.

"Would you prefer..."

"Yes."

"...something stronger?"

"Yes," I said, again. At which point, Sophie produced a bottle of vodka and two glasses. We toasted to the memory of Hyman Pietroski, and Sophie cried some more. After a minute, I screwed up my courage to continue.

"Look," I said. "There was evidence on his body that Hyman was tortured. That tells me he didn't kill himself. I don't know how much of this they might have told you but..."

"The bruises?" she said.

I nodded.

"The burn marks on his nipples?"

I nodded again.

"And the pinky?" Sophie said. "Yes, I know."

"But you still think he killed himself?"

"I know he killed himself."

"But the beating, the burns on his nipples, the pinky that was lopped off — he didn't do that to himself."

"Drink that up," she said, and then she poured us two more and it all began spilling out.

"It all happened so fast when I think about it," she said. "Your meetings were on Thursday nights — yes, he told me. He liked you, by the way. He said he felt calmer after he talked to you. Anyway, he thought he would get the last of the plans he was stealing in the next few days, and you'd have one more meeting, and then it would be over. That's what he told me on Thursday night. We were supposed to have dinner on Friday, but he never showed up — not until after 10 o'clock. He had the bruises then, and the burned nipples, and a big gauze wrap where his pinky used to be."

She stopped. I didn't say anything.

"The UB," Sophie said, and then she poured some more. Even though I had known in my heart that Hyman had been tortured by the UB, the confirmation still hit me. It made no sense, but it did.

"It wasn't you," she said. "It was a guy at his work. Hyman never liked him, and from what he could gather, the guy was keeping more of an eye on Hyman's movements at work than he knew. At a certain point, the guy called the UB — that was what Hyman figured. Because the UB guys picked him up at work, right at the drafting table, and kind of made a reference to someone in his office."

Sophie said that Hyman had no idea where he had been taken. It was about a half-hour drive, but he was guessing. And he was blindfolded for the ride. When they stopped and dragged him out of the car and into a building and then down some steps, he was in a cell of some kind.

"He said he pissed himself, and that was before they even started in on him," she said. "He was so embarrassed about that but he felt like he had to tell me everything."

As she got deeper into the retelling, Sophie stopped crying. It was almost clinical in its detail. The beating first, rubber hoses on his torso and his legs. The electrical leads next, attached on one end to a car battery and the other to his nipples. Then, finally, the pinky.

"He said they had three different sizes of loppers hanging on a pegboard," she said. "Small, medium and tree trunk — that's how he described them. He said they used medium on his pinky. He said he passed out for a minute after that. He said it felt like a minute."

I had questions but didn't dare interrupt. It would have been like breaking into a deathbed confession to ask what the weather was like.

"In the end, he gave up something," she said.

Sophie downed her glass.

"In the end, he gave up you."

I knew it, of course. I knew it deep down. Because the way it worked, the man without a pinky always gave it up in the end — and the only thing Hyman had to give up, when you really thought about it, was me. There were the mechanics — what he had stolen, and the method, and the purpose — and there was value in that for the UB, no doubt. But I was the only human who was part of the equation, and the UB — really any security service — wanted humans most of all.

"He felt terrible," Sophie said.

"He shouldn't have. He was tortured. Nobody survives torture."

"I tried to tell him as much."

"He should have listened to you."

She waved her hand, batting away the notion. The bottle was empty, and Sophie went into a kitchen cupboard for a bottle of red wine.

"They let him go provided he would bring in some new information," she said. Every Thursday, they told him. Between 3 and 5 o'clock. Every Thursday. And, well, he couldn't do it. He worried all week, didn't eat, didn't sleep. He didn't live here, but he did that week. He was just a mess. He just kept saying, 'Not again.' And, 'Why do they keep choosing me?'"

She must have seen a question on my face.

"It goes back to the sonderkommando," she said. "Always the goddamned sonderkommando. When the Nazis put him in that job, it was like a death sentence for Hyman — a mental death sentence. You know what I mean? He could never shake it. He felt guilty about it for no reason. I tried to tell him that. I know his friend Moishe tried to tell him. But he couldn't let it go. And then that young kid recruited him for your thing, and it was more of the same — and it ended up with him with electrodes on his nipples, and with him giving them your name. The guilt, it was overwhelming for him. And he just kept saying it. 'Why do they keep choosing me?'"

At this, Sophie cracked again and began sobbing violently. When I thought about it later, I should have gotten up and embraced her — but it would have been awkward both physically and mentally. So I sat there, and she shook so hard that her hair fell over her face.

"He came home from work a few days later and told me he was thinking about killing himself," she said. "That was the night we spent the whole night talking except for that hour of sleep at the end. I really thought I had gotten through to him, too. When he was leaving the apartment to go to work, I told him I loved him. He stopped at the door and looked back over his shoulder and told me that he loved me, too. And then he broke into a grin and turned and shut the door behind him. Last thing I saw, that grin."

"I hope it's some comfort," I said, and Sophie smiled.

"He never came home for dinner that night. He hanged himself, but you know that."

I nodded.

"It was a Thursday," she said.

PART IV

37

I bought a bottle and took it back to my little room at St. Anne's. It was more a cell than a room, truth be told, but it was fine. Nobody bothered me. The pastor was one of the good guys and knew that I was on a special assignment of some sort. There were two other priests who lived there, and the pastor told them my cover story about taking the course at Jagiellonian University and needing to work long hours in the library besides. The cook made me sandwiches and such and left them on a tray outside my door, which allowed me to skip the group dinner. Breakfast was pretty much fruit and bread and coffee, and I could wolf that down in minutes. I would go days without seeing a soul and would pretend my Polish was worse than it was when forced to converse. The whole thing was easy.

But me and the bottle spent a long night after I left Sophie's apartment. I had come back to Krakow to deal with Dabrowski and his big nose. That was the inciting incident, as they say in the drama course in school. But the deeper reason was the one that had plagued my sleep for months and years. It was the need for an answer to one question: was I the reason that Hyman Pietroski was dead?

The answer I received from Sophie made me feel better — like, 75 percent better. The UB picked up Hyman at work, and there had been a rival of sorts at his company. It made sense that there was something in that rivalry and perhaps a moment of carelessness. Add those two together and the sum is that it was as it seemed. Hyman got himself caught, somehow.

There was that, and another key bit: that they never came after me. If I had been the one who was careless, who opened the door that the UB subsequently walked through, why hadn't they scooped me up, too? To be honest, I was more valuable to the UB than Hyman was. He knew what he was stealing, and that was a fact, but his worth was truly measured in his ability to deliver me to the UB — because my breadth of knowledge, extracted piece by piece with each jolt of electricity delivered to my scrotum, was potentially gold for the Polish security forces. So if they had identified me first and then gone after Hyman, well, that was backwards from a value proposition. If they knew about me first, I would have been arrested first. And the fact that I wasn't arrested first meant that they found out about me from Hyman and not the other way around.

So, 75 percent. It would have been even higher if not for the bottle I was demolishing in my room at St. Anne's. Because the alcohol made me more paranoid than usual, and the paranoia tended to carry me, like a raft on rapids, on an uncontrolled — and uncontrollable — terror ride into the darkest parts of my memory. Specifically, the parts where I thought about that drunken night with the woman, and my pathetic weakness, and my blatant disregard for one of Fritz's basic rules of the undercover life: hookers only.

So, a drunken doom loop in my little cell of a room. So, 75 percent that I sometimes was able to get to 90 percent. But only sometimes.

Even at 75 percent, though, I was torn by conflicting emotions — sadness but also relief. And what kind of an asshole did that make me? What kind of asshole could be oddly happy that Hyman really did get himself caught, and that he really did kill himself, and that he'd given me away to the UB besides?

38

I was wearing my priest's getup, carrying a knapsack that contained exactly one book on philosophy. It was chosen because it was the slimmest volume in the philosophy section of Jagiellonian University library, the lightest to carry. The truth was, I barely knew it was there. The other truth was, I hadn't even bothered to check the title.

My plan was to head over to the café across from St. Andrew's and take another peek at Dabrowski and see if he worked at the school every day. For what reason, I wasn't sure. I was really done with what I had come to do in Krakow, and when you were done, there was no reason to hang around for a minute longer. I had done everything I could to satisfy myself that Hyman Pietroski had gotten himself captured by the UB, that it wasn't my fault — and if I wasn't 100 percent convinced, I was as close as I was ever going to get. And as for Dabrowski, I had laid the trap that would ensnare him — and that was all I could do. Staying in Krakow to see if it worked was foolish. I mean, it wasn't as if the UB was going to send me a telegram of congratulations if they got him.

So, it was time to go. It would be one more look at Dabrowski from a distance, and then out. I got a message to Father Krazinski, and we were to meet at the first café near the train station at two. After the meeting, wearing my priestly disguise — from the cassock to the goofy hat — I would begin my slow exfiltration from Poland, local train by tedious local train. Four days to Swinoujscie, probably, and then a nighttime swim back to Ahlbeck, to Karin, to Lotte. And if I had no idea how I would explain myself to Karin, I had no doubt that I needed to try.

I left St. Anne's by the side door, as usual. The noise from the pigeons hit me as soon as I stepped outside. The old men were feeding the birds on the benches. I had never clocked their faces before, but I did see this time that there was a younger guy among the group. Whatever.

I got to the path and made a left toward St. Andrew's. When I approached the benches and the men, the birds scattered and the younger guy stood up and walked toward the place where the street met the path. The front of the church was that way. So was a public phone box on the corner.

I didn't get another block when I saw two black trench coats emerge from a side street. Shit. Maybe the younger guy feeding the pigeons wasn't heading to the church or the phone box. Maybe the act of standing up was the signal.

I stopped, looked at my watch, opened my knapsack, looked inside, mimed a curse, and began walking back toward the rectory — all as if I had forgotten something. Once inside, well, I had no idea what I would do — but inside seemed to be my safest option. If the only obstacle was the single younger pigeon-feeder, I was confident I could blow past him — unless, of course, he was armed.

My confidence ebbed, though, when I saw two more black trench coats walking toward me from the other direction, and then a black car and another black trench coat parked in front of the church. Running across the grass was my only option, and it seemed silly. So I just stood where I was and waited as the vise of black trench coats tightened.

"Father, after you," one of them said. He pointed toward the car. I walked, and the guy held my elbow and guided me. It wasn't necessary, though. I wasn't resisting.

39

The ride was pleasant enough, as those things went. Wrists shackled in the front, not the back. One black trench coat sitting to my left and one to my right, but it was a big-ass back seat. Comfy, almost.

It wasn't a long ride, maybe 10 minutes. We approached the train station but then headed to the left along a busy street. There were apartments and such on the right and another one of Krakow's seemingly endless stretch of ribbon parks on the left. I had no idea what was on the other side of the trees and no time to guess.

Oddly, I was able — pretty easily — to put out of my mind the bit of business that was about to occur. I had done it before and always survived with nothing more scarring than the nightmares about the electrodes attached to my testicles. Which wasn't nothing but, well...

The key in these situations — starting for me in the Gestapo jail in Cologne in 1938 and ending, well, with that car ride next to the ribbon parks — was having the story prepared ahead of time. I had it this time, too, but I needed to rehearse it in my head one final time. But before I got to the story, all of the details of the last few weeks flashed past in a blink. Still, it seemed as if every detail shone like a diamond in the sunlight.

After observing Big Nose Dabrowski that first night in Feniks, and ruminating/marinating for a day or so, I came up with what I believed to be a workable plan. Every night after that, with my hat pulled down over my eyes, I walked past Feniks and peeked through the window to see if my girl, the hostess, was working. I needed to go on one of her off nights, and it took me two tries before I saw another girl working the door. I told her I was just going for a quick drink at the bar, and she barely looked up as she waved me inside.

I scanned the room: no Dabrowski. Good. After the bartender brought my Manhattan, I set the thing in motion. After 30 seconds about the rainy weather — "The angels won't stop pissing," the bartender said — I got to it.

"Hey, have you seen that little guy with the big nose in here tonight?" I said.

"Nope. Usually Friday or the weekends," the bartender said.

"So you know him?"

"Hard to forget."

"I know. That fucking honker, I mean..."

"If he was taller, you could use it for an umbrella," the bartender said.

We both laughed and told a couple of big nose jokes. Mine was about the lifeguard who cleared the beach in a panic and yelled "Shark! Shark!" only to discover that it was Dabrowski doing the backstroke. The bartender's joke was better, seeing as how it involved cunnilingus. The guy was a riot, and I easily could have spent the evening on that stool, but there was business to be done.

"Besides the nose, have you noticed how handsy he is?" I said.

"No, not so much."

"He's all over you. It's creepy. Pat your arm. Punch your shoulder. Like I said, handsy. It's... I don't know. If I didn't know better..."

We both traded a laugh, and then a leer, and then a kind of fake shiver, and that was it. Big nose, handsy, maybe queer. The seed had been planted. If my new favorite bartender didn't work for the UB, or the NKVD, or both, then they weren't trying as hard as I thought.

Two nights later, I was back at the café across from St. Andrew's. I fortified myself with an entire bottle of the bad red wine. That was to be the night, the most important night, and I did better in those kinds of situations when I was on the edge of intoxication.

Out came Dabrowski, like the last time. He walked through the main square, like the last time. He opened the door to Feniks, like the last time. Now or never.

I was hoping for a different girl out front and a different bartender. The girl was the same, the original, but she barely flirted when I told her I was headed to the bar. The bartender was different, though. It didn't really matter in the end, but it was cleaner with a new person.

Dabrowski was at the far end of the bar, sitting by himself. I acted as if I was surprised to see a familiar face as I walked by.

"Father Dabrowski! All the way from Swinoujscie! Small world," I said.

Dabrowski replied with a blank look and silence.

"Oh, sorry. You're off duty. But, well, I can't believe it's you. I just wanted to say how much I enjoyed your sermons. So meaningful. Such an effortless way of connecting the scripture to a person's daily life."

Dabrowski mumbled some version of thank you.

The bartender edged closer. He was clearly listening.

"Do you see much of your friend, that big redheaded guy? What's his name? Carney? Yeah, I think that's it. Carney."

"I don't know who that is."

"I could have sworn I saw you two together in Swinoujscie. In The Night Watchman. I don't know. I could have sworn. I don't know. I guess I'm mistaken."

Dabrowski said nothing but he looked annoyed.

"Off duty," I said. "I'm an idiot. You work so hard, and you get one night off, and here I am — excuse my forwardness. Please forgive me. Enjoy your evening, Father."

I walked away and managed one quick peek over my shoulder — not at Dabrowski but at the bartender. He had walked to the other end of the bar, away from Dabrowski, and was actually writing something down on the order pad he kept in his apron pocket — except he wasn't taking anyone's order.

I walked out of Feniks without even a half-hearted attempt at banter with the girl up front. I knew then that I couldn't go into Feniks again and that I couldn't see Dabrowski again. I had to hope that the hints I had dropped would be enough. I had to hope that the bartenders were on the UB payroll because if they weren't, I wasn't sure what to do next.

Because despite what Father Krazinski had told me about how his bosses in the Holy Fucking Roman Catholic Church wanted me to eliminate Dabrowski, I wasn't in that business. I had a code, however tattered. So, if I could get him in trouble with the UB, and maybe lead them to believe that he was involved somehow with their comrade — the very dead, very redheaded Carney — I was fine with that. But do it myself? No. Two murders in two weeks? No.

40

After 10 minutes, the car pulled to a curb. The street sign said we were on Plac Inwalidow. We were between two buildings, No. 3 and No. 4. As I stood on the sidewalk between my two minders, the one on the left said, "Which one is his office in?" The one on the right pointed, and the three of us marched into No. 3.

Second floor, front room, looking out over the street. They pointed me to a chair and then stood on either side. After a few minutes, a head poked in and said, "Take the cuffs off, he isn't going anywhere. I'll be back in a minute." I couldn't see the guy through my minder on the right. Quickly, the shackles were unlocked, and I massaged my wrists and waited. And if I was scared as hell on the one hand, I was at least a little bit relaxed, too. We were only in an office, after all. What was he going to do, beat me senseless with the drawer from a file cabinet?

Two minutes became five, and five became 10, and then the same head that I couldn't see poked into the door, and the same voice spoke:

"You know what? Take him to the other place. I'm more comfortable there. The key is in my top right drawer."

As it turned out, the other place was about two blocks away on Pomorska. No. 2. We got inside and, well, let's just say we weren't in an office anymore. There were no file cabinets. Instead, there were the time-honored implements of information gathering: knives and loppers in various sizes hung from a pegboard, and three car batteries sat on a table with electric leads right beside them.

And then there was the writing on the wall. They just left it there, unafraid and unashamed that it would be discovered. Same as Cologne. And if I felt the sight of the battery in my sphincter, the words on the wall pierced my heart.

This one stood out:

Dearest Mummy
And Daddy and my dear family, will I
See you
Again?
God only knows
In since VIII.1
Say farewell to the family

And, this one:

The only witnesses
To the tears shed
And the goings-on in here
Are these four walls
And good Jesus

I was staring at the words when the same voice from the office interrupted my thoughts.

"That wasn't us," he said. "That was the fucking Gestapo. Not us. I always think it's important to point out. I mean, I think I'm the only one who uses this place. We have cells in the basement below my office, and the citizens of Krakow all know about them. They call our building 'the torture house' or 'the death factory.' That's an overstatement, but we don't bother correcting it. That place, it has its purpose. But, I don't know. I prefer to work over here sometimes. I'm pretty sure I have the only key."

He stopped.

"Where are my manners?" he said. "I haven't introduced myself. My name is Captain Piotr Kandinsky. And you are Father Alex Kovacs."

He held up a rolled-up piece of paper and also my passport. They were in my knapsack along with the philosophy book.

"I feel better now," Kandinsky said. In the next room, a telephone began to ring. Kandinsky looked at my two minders.

"Stripped to the waist and shackled," he said.

"But, Captain," the one said, gesturing up and down at the line of buttons holding my cassock together.

Kandinsky laughed and said, "Yes, it's a new one for me, too. Undo the buttons halfway down, then, and get his arms out of the thing."

Kandinsky left the room while the two of them did as instructed. The phone stopped ringing and I could hear one side of a muffled conversation. The trench coats got my arms out of the sleeves, sat me on a metal table, and locked my wrists and my ankles into place. Again, I didn't resist.

41

"So, Father Alex Kovacs," Kandinsky said.

I nodded.

"Here from Prague to attend a seminar at Jagiellonian University."

I nodded again.

"A seminar that doesn't exist," he said.

I stared.

"Anything to say for yourself?"

"As my papers show…"

"Fuck your papers and fuck you. Unbutton the rest of that getup and yank down his drawers. My papers. Jesus. Fuck your papers."

The trench coats did as they were instructed. They tossed the cassock in a heap on the floor. I was still wearing my shoes and socks, and my underpants were down around my ankles. The metal table was cold. Somehow, amid my growing panic, that feeling registered.

While they worked, Kandinsky walked over to the table holding the three car batteries. I hadn't noticed the wheels before. It was really a cart, and the good captain steered it over so that it was right next to the table where my naked ass currently resided.

"Anything to say?" Kandinsky said. He was putting on a pair of thick rubber gloves as he spoke.

"About what?"

"About what you are really doing in our fair country, Father Alex Kovacs?"

"As my papers say, I am attending—"

"Enough. Fuck it. I don't have time for your bullshit today."

He pulled the gloves a bit farther onto his hands. He spread his fingers and admired them.

"Nipples for some, balls for you," Kandinsky said. "Yes, balls for you."

With a swift motion, he snatched up one of the electric leads — it had a little gold clip on the end — and attached the clip to my ballsack. I didn't feel the pinch. I did, though, think I was going to faint.

Kandinsky stepped back, inspecting his handiwork. Then he reached down and picked up the other end of the wire. He held it up so I could see it — my eyes must have been bugged out — and then he began to lower it toward one of the battery terminals. He held it, I don't know, maybe six inches away.

"Last chance, Mr. Alex Kovacs..."

Panicked, I gave him something. This wasn't how I had planned it. I thought they would start with a few kidney punches and work from there. A beating, maybe a pinky. I thought I could sacrifice a pinky for the sake of the story. I figured there would be a progression so that when I finally gave it up, it would seem more real. That I had demonstrated a level of resistance. Here, I was just fucking folding before I had even taken any cards. It was too quick. But my fear of an electric wire clipped to my balls was too real, too longstanding. I knew I should wait for at least one jolt but I couldn't.

What I said — more of a high-pitched yelp — was, "Father Dabrowski. Father Dabrowski."

"Interesting. What about Father Dabrowski, Father Dabrowski?" Kandinsky mimicked my pathetic voice when he repeated the name.

I paused. Thought I was going to pass out.

"Catch your breath, Alex Kovacs. Catch your breath and tell me about Father Dabrowski."

I took a deep breath and I wondered if this was going to hold together. Normally, I would spend days on concocting a story like this. Before a mission, Fritz and I would sit for hours and hours and game out this type of conversation. I could only hope, with the lead still clipped to my ballsack, that all of those previous rehearsals had prepared me. I had laid the groundwork at Feniks, but I was winging this conversation. I had kind of planned it, but not fully.

"It's just that, the people you think you know well, sometimes you don't," I said

"Go ahead. I'm intrigued."

"People have secrets."

"Too cryptic, Alex Kovacs."

He picked up the lead, took a step toward me, and waved it under my nose.

"He drinks, you know."

"A priest who drinks? Alert the media. It's an occupational hazard. So?"

"At the Feniks here in Krakow. He drinks a lot."

"Yes, yes. Tell me something I don't know."

"He drinks a lot at Feniks, and he talks a lot after he drinks a lot. And, well, from what he says, there's another place he drinks — or drank, I guess — in Swinoujscie. The Night Watchman. Ever hear of it?"

Kandinsky put down the lead, dragged a wooden chair over to sit right in front of me.

"And?" he said.

"Well, your Father Dabrowski. Let's just say he took care of more than that Father Sciabotski in Swinoujscie. That was his name, right? Father Piotr Sciabotski?"

The UB captain smiled.

"Okay, I'm officially impressed," he said.

I paused.

"More," he said.

"He says he drank at The Night Watchman in Swinoujscie. And he says there was this security police officer — a counterpart of yours, I would guess. I don't know how your force is organized. But would you know names?"

"I might," he said.

"Carney," I said.

Kandinsky didn't react. I kept talking.

"Well, he says he was drinking one night at The Night Watchman. And he says he was there to meet a security police officer. Like you, maybe. Carney. But he said it was 'unofficial.' And he said it with a leering wink."

"The fuck?"

"I was surprised, too. I mean, I didn't even know him, and he's telling me this. Really, so drunk. I mean, he had already begun patting me on the back after saying something he thought was funny. Like, weirdly familiar patting on the back. I mean, I don't know, but…"

Pause.

"I guess I played along," I said.

Pause.

"And?"

"And he told me the story of a night in Swinoujscie when he

left The Night Watchman with the security police officer. And they went down by the river. And they, well, they began — until the officer, well, balked. And threatened your Father Dabrowski with exposure. Except, well, he was doing the threatening while his pants were down around his ankles. And he tripped. And your Father Dabrowski, he hit him on the back of the head with a rock."

"This is bullshit..."

"That's what I thought. But he was crying when he told me. I mean, it was... I couldn't believe he was telling me. But he was so drunk, and I guess I had played along, and he thought he saw something, I don't know, a kindred spirit. I mean, he really was crying. We were by ourselves in a back booth, and he was wiping his face on his sleeve, when somebody came up and shouted his name. Two friends of his. I was able to slip out after that."

Arms folded, the UB captain took in everything I had said. He was silent for maybe 30 seconds, which seemed like 30 minutes. Then he waved the wire under my nose and smiled.

"You were never in danger, you know," Kandinsky said. "Your balls, I mean. Never in danger. Well, not after that phone call."

My face must have betrayed a question.

"The call, it was from the chancery," he said. "Office of the Archbishop. The biggest of the big shits. It appears that someone saw you being, well, invited to see me outside of that church where you were living. And the Office of the Archbishop was calling to request a courtesy for a visiting scholar at Jagiellonian University."

Kandinsky stopped and laughed. Quickly, softly. Then he waved his hand.

"We are not big fans of your archbishop," he said. "I'm sure the feeling is mutual. He doesn't like us, and we don't like him. Fine. But the thing is, well, let's just say that we have hope for some of his potential replacements. He's not a young man, after all. And so, well, I guess we're going to play nice for now. Professional courtesy, as they say. The Archbishop is your theoretical boss..."

With that, Kandinsky tossed my paperwork and my passport onto the metal table where I was sitting with the electric wire still very much attached to my ballsack.

"He's your, ahem, boss, and I have bosses, too," Kandinsky said. "And this is their call, my bosses. Not how I would have played it, but..."

His voice trailed off, and then Kandinsky stood up, unclipped me, tossed the wire onto the table, and slowly tugged the thick rubber gloves from his hands.

"You understand, I'm sure, that your quote-unquote course of study is over," he said.

I nodded.

"By tomorrow," he said.

I nodded again.

"Let him go," Captain Kandinsky said, over his shoulder, as he left the room.

42

Kandinsky said I had until the next day, but I wasn't going to take any chances. I still had time to get to the café near the train station and meet with Father Krazinski, and I would keep the meeting mostly to try to understand what had just happened from his end. Oh, and to warn him that the Commies had a couple of favored successors to the current archbishop. He probably already knew, or at least suspected, but whatever. One beer and then across the street and into the station and onto the next local train heading northeast toward Szczecin.

I got myself buttoned up while the two trench coats studied their fingernails, and then my knapsack and I were out. No one said anything and no one followed me. I kept expecting someone to stop me on the stairs but no one did.

I mean, it was true that I had told Kandinsky a story of some value. He could now scoop up Dabrowski and maybe sweat him a little bit — you know, put the shoe on the other foot or, in this case, the electrical wire on the other ballsack. He might get something out of it. Or he might just stitch up Dabrowski for

Carney's murder in Swinoujscie and call it an afternoon. Either way, a win for the UB.

But Kandinsky never asked me the question for which I had no answer. That is, what the fuck was I doing in Poland in the first place?

Maybe it was as simple as Kandinsky said, that his bosses wanted to do a solid for the archbishop in the hope that the old man might put his thumb on the scale, at least a little bit, when it came to suggesting his successor to the pope. Playing the long game, so to speak. I guess it made as much sense as anything. Maybe Krazinski would know more.

I got to the sidewalk outside of Pomorska 2, and it took me a second to orient myself. Up to the corner and then which way? Left. Yeah, left — past the other UB offices where I first sat and then toward the train station. I was guessing it would be about a half-hour walk, give or take, provided I didn't get too lost. I'd have the one drink with Krazinski and then get to the station. I'd load up on sandwiches and get a bottle of vodka — beers would be too heavy — and make my way. I was pretty sure I'd be able to retrace my steps and duplicate the sequence of trains back to Swinoujscie. Then Karin and Lotte. For some reason, the picture of the ice cream cone dripping on my finger jumped into my head, and I couldn't help but grin as I walked.

As I got to Plac Inwalidow, the street where the UB headquarters was, I could feel my face fall. At the corner, just a few feet from the UB building, there was someone who quite obviously was waiting for me. It took me a second to make the connection, but only a second. I knew the face but it was out of context, like when you see your plumber at the green grocer. A second, but only a second.

The last time I had seen her, she had been asleep. The covers on her bed had been askew, and one of her breasts had been peeking out. I had seen her drunk and I had seen her hungover in the early dawn — never clear-eyed, never in bright light. But it was her. There was no doubt.

Only this time, she was wearing a uniform.

43

"Took a second, didn't it?" she said.

I didn't answer.

"Relax, the car will be here in a second."

I made a face.

"He doesn't know," she said, and then added a wave in the direction of the cells on Pomorska, the cells where Captain Kandinsky had just teased me. "He won't like it, but some things are above his pay grade."

What was she going to do? Kill me? And what was this all about?

"I can see the questions on your face. So many questions. Go ahead, we have a little time."

She looked at her watch.

"A little time. Go ahead, ask away. At this point, you knowing won't matter much either way."

I didn't know what to say or where to begin.

"Back then," I said. "Just a coincidence?"

"There are no coincidences in this line of work," she said. "You know that, I'm sure. Your command of the Polish language was OK, but not native, clearly. That and the German accent —

even ordering a beer, a bartender can pick that up. And if every bartender in Krakow isn't on our payroll at this point, well, it's at least every other bartender."

"So, you came looking for me? From some bartender's information?"

"Wasn't hard to find you."

"Or entice me."

"You were drunk," she said. "I'm 10 years younger than you. What's the American saying? Like shooting fish in a barrel?"

"But I didn't tell you anything," I said. "At least, I don't think I told you anything. I was pretty fucked up. You too, if I remember correctly."

"Socially drunk, not fucked up. There's a significant difference. It's one of the skills they teach you. Anyway, you didn't tell me anything. You didn't need to."

"Then what?"

"Your jacket. While you slept."

"There was nothing in my jacket."

"Nothing but a nicely hidden compartment beneath the lining," she said. "Not just a rip in the lining, but the work of a seamstress with an affection for espionage. We followed you everywhere after that. Big debate in the office. Your boy over there…"

She pointed again toward Pomorska 2.

"Kandinsky."

"Fucking Kandinsky — that's my first name for him," she said. "Anyway, he thought it was a waste. Fought me hard. Called me a drunken skirt to the boss. But I convinced him. We had one guy follow you from my building that morning — that was happening either way — but the fight was over the next days. It ended up being a six-man team. Cost a fortune."

Finally, the car pulled up. There were two guys in the front. The passenger got out and opened the back door. He told me to get in, and he handcuffed both of my hands to a handle on the back seat. The chains were long enough to be somewhat comfortable but short enough that I couldn't reach the front seat.

"It's a long ride, so try to relax," she said.

I just looked at her.

"No sense fighting it," she said, and then she slammed the door.

The car roared off. I realized then that I didn't know her name. I also realized that I hadn't asked her the question that I had come to Krakow to answer. That is: was I the reason that the UB captured Hyman Pietroski?

It still made no sense that they would nab him before me because I was honestly the much more valuable target. But now I had confirmation that I had indeed screwed up when I broke Fritz's cardinal rule, and that my senses had been correct when I thought I was being followed. Even if it made no sense, it was all there. And, well, fuck.

Still, I forced myself to concentrate. I had been in the city often enough to know vaguely where we were headed — north, south, east or west — and we were going north. They didn't blindfold me and, over the hours, I could see the names of some of the little towns as we drove through. I recognized several of them, and it took me a second to realize why, but then I did. They were train stops on the way toward Swinoujscie.

44

Other than two piss breaks along the side of the road, plus another stop where I was permitted 10 minutes to wolf down a sandwich while leaning against the car's front fender, we drove straight through. It was still the middle of the night when we arrived at the destination. It was as I had suspected for hours. It was Swinoujscie.

I recognized a lot of it — not on the outskirts but when we entered the city proper. That was all I had ever seen, after all. We drove within about three blocks of Stella Maris, and then we were right along the beach promenade. That's where the car pulled to a stop.

"Relax," the driver said. "We're early. You can rest your eyes — it's not for an hour. We made good time."

The two of them rolled down their windows and seemed to settle back in their seats, closing their eyes themselves. It was a dark night, cloudy. I could hear the Baltic off to my right, lapping against the shore.

I had no idea what was happening. The woman back in Krakow and my two minders in the front seat had been relaxed beyond reason. It was as if I was just another item on their to-do list: butter, milk, eggs, Kovacs. That calmed me in a way, but only a little. My best guess, given the geography, was that I was about to be handed over to the Stasi and their own car batteries with wires attached. I spoke German. Maybe poor Piotr Sciabotski had given me up to the UB, and the connection had only recently been made between the Swinoujscie branch of the intelligence business and the Krakow branch, and it had been decided that delivering me to the Stasi was more valuable than making nice with the old archbishop. There was no way to know, but nothing else really made sense as I sat there in the back of the car and listened to the little waves that intermittently broke the silence of the night.

It was almost exactly an hour later when the driver stirred from his nap, lit a match, looked at his wristwatch, and said, "Five minutes." That woke the other guy, who looked over his shoulder at me, and then at my manacles, and then turned back forward and rubbed his eyes.

Then, he said to the driver, "Tell me again about sleep."

"We're here all day, then one night in the hotel. The Prince's Inn. Then start back in the morning."

"Two rooms?"

"These cheap bastards? Are you kidding?"

"But we still have the night," the passenger said. It was at that point that each of them revealed the name of a different whorehouse they had gotten from their friends. They then spent several minutes arguing about which was the better recommendation, with the driver finally concluding, "Fuck it. We have time for both. Do you have money for both?"

The passenger was about to answer when a pair of headlights flicked on in the distance.

"Showtime," the driver said. He turned on his headlights in reply.

They got out of the car. The passenger opened the back door, leaned in, and unlocked the shackles. He stood on the pavement and watched me rub my wrists for a few seconds before saying, "Any day now, asshole. Are you waiting for an engraved fucking invitation?"

I got out of the car, and then the three of us stood in front with the headlights at our backs. The other headlights were probably 300 feet away. Maybe 400. Within a few seconds, there were two people standing in front of those headlights. This would be the handoff, then. I hadn't been wrong.

The three of us began walking, and the two of them began walking. Lights shining behind us, lights blinding in front of us, it made for an eerie scene in the darkness that was accentuated by the canopy of trees over the promenade.

We were approaching the border. I recognized that much. We were on the Polish side, and we were almost to the guard shack and the gate — red stripes on white wood — that they lowered and raised after checking your papers. Just past the shack was the new death strip. You could see the beach dunes off to the right. For some reason, I became fixated at just how long the shadows were as my captors and I reached the wooden gate.

We stood there for maybe 30 seconds, and then a guard came out of the shack and raised the gate.

"Just walk," the driver said.

I walked. With my first step, I could see the gate on the East German side also opened. I could see that and I also could see a guard with a rifle, just like his Polish counterpart. I looked right, then left. The land had been completely cleared of vegetation. The trees had been cut down to stumps. There was nowhere to run.

That's when I noticed the two people walking toward me from the East German side. We were going to meet in the middle of the death strip, it seemed. And then, well, fuck.

The stretch of the promenade still was not lit up. There was only the light from the car headlights — lights and shadows behind me, lights in my eyes ahead of me. We were maybe 100 feet apart when I realized that one of the two men on the East German side had stopped walking while the other continued on. And then it was all kind of a numb blur for me as 100 feet became 50, and 50 became 25, and the lights and the shadows and the tiny waves on the Baltic and...

We were maybe five feet apart when I saw.

It was Gus.

I paused for a second when I recognized my friend from The Denkler, but he did not. I had drunk with him, consoled him, killed that redheaded animal Carney for him, but he never broke stride. I almost said something and got the first word half out of my mouth, but then it caught in my throat. It came out as a grunt more than anything, not that Gus heard. He just kept walking. He did not look me in the eye.

After passing him, I turned and looked over my shoulder, but he did not. I just saw the back of him — that and the headlights from the car I had just left. And my mouth must have been wide open when I reached the other man, the one who had stopped walking while Gus continued on.

That was when Fritz said, "In the car. I'll try to explain."

45

No words, not for a couple of minutes. Just the bottle that Fritz had handed me, and the sound of my gulp, and the wiping of my sleeve along my chin, the fabric scratching across the unshaven skin. And then another gulp.

We drove up the promenade, where no one ever drove except for about two blocks in the middle of Ahlbeck and a few more in the middle of Heringsdorf. The promenade was for walking — hence the name. It was still late enough, or early enough, that there was no one out. When we reached Ahlbeck, we turned into the town and came within about two blocks of my apartment, four blocks of Karin and Lotte's. But the engine roared through the night, and I barely looked. I knew we weren't going to be stopping.

About five minutes after that, it was pretty obvious to me what our destination was.

"Berlin?" I said.

Fritz nodded. He reached for the bottle, took his first sip, and handed it back.

"I... I..."

"You don't know where to begin?" Fritz said. "Let me help you. Gus was on to you. That's how this all started."

I didn't see how that was possible, not from anything I had done. Well, at least not anything I had done in Heringsdorf or Ahlbeck.

"Was it the girl in Krakow who gave me to him?" I said. "You know about her?"

"The UB girl?"

I nodded and my eyes dropped. "Hookers only" was the mantra. He knew it, and I knew it, and if I broke the rules sometimes — and he knew I did — it didn't keep him from repeating the admonition. Still, he said nothing, not this time. No recriminations. No I-told-you-so.

"No, not the UB girl," Fritz said. No I-told-you-so, but he did allow me to marinate in my recklessness for a few seconds.

"No, not her," he said. "It was more complicated than that. It was the hooker from The Denkler. She ratted you out to Gus."

"What? Micky?"

"If that's her name."

"That is her name, but she didn't know anything about me. I mean, about all of this."

"She found out."

"How?"

"Gluck, your contact," Fritz said.

"The big oaf? What about him?"

"He got a little sweet on your Micky, you know, after his monthly visits to collect the intel from you at the bar."

"I never noticed."

"Well, there you have it. He's in a prison cell right now, outside of Munich. Gehlen himself is trying to figure out what to do with him. Fucking Gluck. Anyway, he got a little too drunk one night, and he must have told Micky enough of what you were up to — and she told Gus."

"But why? She had nothing against me."

"It had nothing to do with you," Fritz said. "It was Gus. She was scared of him. She thought he was Stasi, mostly because he told her he was Stasi. And I mean, given that, it's not like she had much of a choice."

"So?" I said.

"So, she told him you were sneaking across the border every month to gather intelligence. Gluck didn't know about the priest, so he couldn't tell Micky that bit. But you and the border, she did have that part. Which meant that Gus Braun had that part. And he was UB."

"He was UB? But he fucking hated the Poles," I said.

"So he told you," Fritz said.

46

We had cleared the line of little towns along the Baltic and were driving on a decent-sized road that was empty. The engine was roaring, and the two of us needed to raise our voices almost to a shout at times.

"So, your good friend Gus," Fritz said. "He took his new trove of information and went to work. The next month, he followed you and saw you sneaking across the border. And then, the next month, he followed you a second time."

"And you know that how?" I said.

"He told us, readily. Happily."

"Why would he do that?"

"Because I was saving his ass," Fritz said.

"I don't get it," I said.

Fritz went on to explain the mechanics. He quickly became aware of two facts — that my priest in Swinoujscie was very much dead, and that I was very much absent from my job behind the lobby bar at The Denkler. The Gehlen contacts in the Polish clergy found out I was in Krakow. That was when he began to create my escape hatch, unbeknownst to me.

"A three-cushion billiard shot" is how Fritz explained it.

First, he approached Gus Braun and gave him a choice: tell me everything or I'll hand you over to the Stasi.

"So, readily and happily," I said. Fritz nodded.

Next, he approached a Stasi counterpart. Fritz was second in command at the Gehlen Org, and he found a man of similar stature for a chat.

"It works like that?" I said.

"At the highest levels, yes," Fritz said. "We're enemies but we're gentlemen, too."

And so, gentleman to gentleman, Fritz let it be known that he knew of a UB agent working in East Germany, and that he could get him out of the country and out of the Stasi's hair for a price.

"The price being a trade," I said.

"Correct. But they didn't have to give up anything. All the Stasi had to do was allow for safe passage. They readily agreed."

"But why would they do that? What was in it for them?"

"Think about it," Fritz said. "It was really a pretty easy decision on their part, mostly because it was easier to sweep something like that under the carpet than cause a big mess by arresting a Polish spy on East German soil. The two countries, they're supposed to be allies — brothers in scientific socialism and all that horseshit. You make an arrest like that, a friendly spy in your backyard, and suddenly the biggest bosses have to be involved — hell, the party would have had to have been involved, it would have been a whole thing. Much easier my way. My counterpart, he saw it immediately.

"So, I had all of that in my back pocket if I needed it," Fritz said. "And, as it turned out, I did."

47

We each took a long drink from the bottle, and then Fritz tapped the driver on the shoulder and we pulled over for a leak.

"Take five minutes here," I said, after we had buttoned up. "Like, so we don't have to scream at each other. Take me back to Gus. What exactly did he do after he found out about me? Do you know?"

"Yeah, yeah," Fritz said. "After he had seen what you were up to, well, he had a radio. He got word to the UB, predicting your next move. He watched you leave your apartment in the middle of the night, and he radioed that it was on. They followed you, followed you to the church. The time, the amount of time you spent in the church — they put two and two together."

"And you know this because..."

"Because Gus told us."

"Readily."

"Happily," Fritz said. "Come on, let's go. It's a long enough drive as it is."

We resumed yelling over the engine's roar.

"The UB, they already suspected the priest," Fritz said.

"They'd seen him before when he was out wandering around town. They didn't make much of it, but his name was in their books. You were the confirmation. But then, totally separate from that, they had a man, a UB man, get killed. They didn't know for sure, didn't know what was what. But your priest..."

"My priest killed the guy," I said.

"He told you?"

"It was like I was hearing his confession."

"Yeah, well, anyway, that's what Gus figured — that the priest did it," Fritz said. "So did the UB. They weren't sure but they figured. And, anyway, while the UB bosses in Swinoujscie were trying to figure out how to handle the priest, a couple of their guys — friends of the dead guy — got drunk one night and came upon the priest out reading his prayer book under a streetlight, and they snatched him. And..."

"Killed him."

Fritz nodded.

"Unauthorized?"

Fritz nodded again.

"Did he?"

"Yeah, they tortured him enough that he admitted it," Fritz said.

"So it was just kind of dumb luck on their part, guessing that it was the priest?" I said.

Fritz shrugged.

"And Dabrowski? The big-nosed priest? He didn't have anything to do with it?"

"Useful idiot, we think," Fritz said. "But it doesn't seem like he got your priest killed. He was nosing around, you should excuse the expression, and he had a UB contact, but that doesn't make him unusual. The Catholic Church in Poland, well, let's just say that the priests fall on both sides of the Communist question."

"I heard as much in Krakow."

"That priest in Krakow, he fucking saved your ass, by the way," Fritz said.

"Krazinski?"

"Yeah. He got the word to us after you were arrested, and he stalled them with some bullshit request from the archbishop. We had already prepped him, and when you were picked up, he got the word to us and we made the deal with the UB for the trade."

"All in, what, two hours? Three?" I said.

"Maybe less," Fritz said.

I whistled.

"Saved your ass," Fritz said, again.

48

There were still so many loose ends, and I seemed incapable of keeping them in any kind of order, chronological or otherwise. So I just kept asking random questions, and Fritz kept fielding them.

"What about Carney?" I said.

"Remind me," Fritz said.

"The redheaded rapist."

"That was you, then?"

I nodded.

"Gus laughed when he told us that one — like, nearly pissed himself."

"So the story about his wife and daughter?"

"Was bullshit," Fritz said. "Never married. Never had a daughter. But Fritz hated the guy forever. And the guy was a rapist, and it disgusted Gus. And he was hoping, if he planted the seed with you…"

"So I'm that easy to play?" I said.

Fritz waved his hand.

"One good thing about that mess," he said. "We know Carney was Gus's rival. Carney's UB bosses don't. We know Gus got Carney killed, using you as his weapon. His bosses don't. It will give us a bit of leverage with him in the future. You know, if he misses his first meeting..."

I raised an eyebrow.

"Yeah, Gus Braun still works for them but he also works for us now," Fritz said.

"So if the UB doesn't know that I killed Carney, who do they think did it?" I said.

"They actually think it was the big-nosed priest. At least, that's me reading between the lines — but it's my best professional guess."

"I did that," I said, and then I explained about the web I wove at Feniks to ensnare Dabrowski. Fritz whistled when I was done.

"Well, you did well there," he said. "And between that and his drunken proclivities, it appears that Big Nose is now a full-fledged UB informant and not just a useful idiot."

I suddenly felt spent, between the night without sleep, and the ebbing adrenaline, and whatever was in the bottle that Fritz had provided. I must have slept for at least a little while because, when a bump in the road startled me, I noticed we weren't in the hinterland anymore. Not in Berlin proper, but there were more houses and whatnot.

"I meant to tell you," Fritz said. "The last time you went over the border, you apparently lost them. Gus watched you leave your place on the night — he had your pattern down — and he radioed back, but they didn't pick you up."

I explained about the fishing boat and the dinghy. Fritz nodded.

"Well, they didn't spot you," he said.

"Well, if that's the case, how did they re-find me in Krakow if they didn't even know I was in the country? And if they didn't know I'd killed Carney?" I said.

"It had to do with that phony priest paperwork they filled out for you," he said. "As it turns out, the UB, they really do check it. And they really do go through the passport and take a photo of the photo. And your girlfriend..."

"Hardly my girlfriend," I said.

"Whatever. She was doing her weekly flip through the photo file and recognized you. That set the whole thing in motion."

The whole thing. I had gone to Krakow to avenge the killing of Father Piotr Sciabotski by taking care of Dabrowski. As it turned out, while I succeeded, Dabrowski apparently had nothing to do with Sciabotski's death.

So, I whiffed there. The other reason I went back to Krakow, the real reason, the reason that had haunted me every time I turned off the lights at night, was Hyman Pietroski.

Or, as I finally asked Fritz, "Did I get the Jewish guy killed because I slept with her?"

"Your girlfriend?"

"Knock it off. Please."

"Fine, fine," Fritz said. "The question you ask, well, I'm not sure — and, really, there's no way to know. No way for us to know. But I can tell you that there was somebody at his work who suspected him, apparently, and that's where he was arrested. That makes the most sense to me."

I wasn't sure if I believed Fritz — I mean, how could he know about somebody at work suspecting Pietroski? But I didn't ask. And if I wasn't sure I believed him, well, that doesn't mean I didn't try. The truth was I had to try.

49

We were in the city when I got to the last bit, the most important bit.

"So, are you going to tell me?"

"What?"

"Where are Karin and Lotte?" I said.

He was looking at some paperwork in the early morning light. When I said their names, he looked up, took off his reading glasses, and cradled them in his right hand.

"They're safe," Fritz said. "We went to them — well, not we. I did it personally. I knew it would be important to you. So, me. I went and I explained to her why we had to relocate her and the little girl."

"What? Why?" I said.

"Think about it," Fritz said. "Gus Braun knew all about you, which means the UB now knows all about you. Between him and whatever the dead priest might have given up — did he know about Ahlbeck or Heringsdorf?"

I nodded.

"So, there you go," Fritz said. "The UB needs a favor from the Stasi one day, offers up Karin and Lotte in exchange for whatever — come on, you get it. They might not even need a favor. They might have a reciprocal arrangement when it comes to that kind of information. You understand, right?"

"I don't know that I do," I said.

"Well, Karin understood. She got it immediately. As it turned out, she really didn't take that much convincing at all. They packed two bags, and we sent a car, and that was that."

I tried to picture them. Karin's face would be hard, determined, betraying nothing. But Lotte? I thought of the bewilderment, of the fear, and I found myself wiping a single tear.

"When Karin agreed, she said there was one condition," Fritz said.

"What?"

"That we not tell you where they are," he said.

"But—"

He shook his head.

"Fritz, come on," I said.

"No," he said. Softly. Sadly, it seemed, but firmly and finally.

ENJOY THIS BOOK? YOU CAN REALLY HELP ME OUT.

The truth is that, even as an author who has sold more than 300,000 books, it can be hard to get readers' attention. But if you have read this far, I have yours – and I could use a favor.

Reviews from people who liked this book go a long way toward convincing future readers of its worth. It won't take five minutes of your time, but it would mean a lot to me. Long or short, it doesn't matter.

Thanks!

I hope you enjoyed *Nightmare in Poland,* the 14th installment in the Alex Kovacs thriller series. I have also written books in two other series. One begins with *A Death in East Berlin* and features a protagonist named Peter Ritter, a young murder detective in East Berlin at the time of the building of the Berlin Wall. The other is the story of a Paris mob family in the late 1950s, beginning with *Conquest.*

Those books, as well as the rest of all three series, are available for purchase now. You can find the links to all of my books at https://www.amazon.com/author/richardwake.

And if you have any interest in joining my reading group and receiving a free novella, *Ominous Austria,* you can do that here: https://dl.bookfunnel.com/g6ifz027t7

Thanks for your interest!

Printed in Dunstable, United Kingdom